aug 1 - 80

THE SMOKING MIRROR

Recent books by Helen McCloy

THE SMOKING MIRROR

A Novel of Suspense

Helen McCloy

DODD, MEAD & COMPANY, NEW YORK

1   2   3   4   5   6   7   8   9   10

Library of Congress Cataloging in Publication Data

McCloy, Helen.
   The smoking mirror.

   I. Title.
PZ3.M13358So   [PS3525.A1587]   813'.5'2   78–16126
ISBN 0–396–07596–7

Contents

He was too much of a gambler not to accept Fate. With him life was at best an uncertain game, and he always recognized the usual percentage in favor of the dealer.

—Bret Harte, "The Outcasts of Poker Flat"

Part One

NORMANDY

May 1940

1
The Pier

He was standing with a policeman at his elbow just inside the gate of the customs' shed. He was French and official. Dark, shapely overcoat, pale gray gloves, and hard felt hat were the official uniform in the France of 1940.

Celia wondered why he was here.

The policeman whispered to her, "Monsieur l'Inspecteur must see all passports coming off the English boat tonight."

She held out her own passport, sure that anything signed by an American secretary of state would pass muster anywhere.

He turned the pages slowly, reading each one, then snapped it shut and dropped it in his overcoat pocket. "If mademoiselle will have the goodness to to wait for a few moments. . . ."

She was so surprised she answered his French in English. "But . . . why . . . ?"

"Wait, if you please."

He was still speaking French, so she went on in French

3

herself. "I must get to Paris tonight and . . ."

Her voice died. He was already looking at the joint passport of the couple in line behind her.

Every pair of eyes in that line was fixed upon her now. How many Parisian dinner tables would be regaled this evening with tales about a dangerous woman criminal who was detained by police on the pier at Dieppe? What could she have been smuggling? Diamonds? Dope?

Not one of them would have believed that she had no more idea of why she was being detained than they had.

Last in line was a young man, tall and thin. She could hardly see his face. He wore his hat tipped forward so that a half-mask of shadow lay across his eyes. He carried his head high with a touch of arrogance. He wore no overcoat, but the May evening was warm enough to excuse that.

As he came face to face with the Inspector, he made a little gesture of negation, hands held apart, a wide space between them. It was then she noticed that his jacket cuffs were threadbare. She was unused to a combination of arrogance and poverty. She found it rather appealing.

"Passport?" The Inspector was curt.

French cadences flowed from the young man almost like poetry, but it all boiled down to the fact that his passport had been stolen.

"When did this happen, monsieur?"

"I had it in my hip pocket when I got on the boat in Newhaven. Just now I looked and it was no longer there."

"Anything else gone?"

"No, fortunately my wallet was in my breast pocket."

"Nationality?"

4

"I have—had—a Nansen passport."

"You are a stateless person?"

"I was born in Russia. My parents brought me out in 1918 when I was one year old."

He glanced towards Celia as he spoke. For the first time she saw his eyes—haunted eyes. How could it be else if you were a second-generation exile? She had known others like him with no memory of their homeland and no thought of counterrevolution, just people trying to come to terms with the times under a handicap.

"Your name?"

"Sergei Radetzkoy."

Celia ventured into French again. "Can't all these things be sorted out when we get to Paris?"

The Inspector rattled off a volley of French at machine-gun speed. At that pace she could not understand a syllable.

"Pardon, monsieur?"

He took a deep breath and tried again, still in French but now with a long pause between each word as if that would help her to understand.

"You . . . speak . . . French?"

"A bit."

"A . . . *little* . . . bit."

This was one lesson in French style she would never forget. Perhaps the best way to learn a language was to get in trouble with the police.

The Inspector now lengthened the pause between each of his words.

"You . . . do . . . not . . . have . . . a . . . visa . . . from . . . the French . . . consul . . . in . . . England."

"Visa?"

The Russian intervened. "Permit me, monsieur?" He

5

went on in English as fluent as his French. If she had not known he was Russian, she would have taken him for an Englishman.

"You're supposed to get a visa from the French consul in London if you are coming from there to enter France. Apparently you didn't."

"Oh, dear, I forgot. Is it important?"

"That depends. Are you a tourist only here for a week or so?"

"No, I'm applying for a job in the Paris office of an American newspaper feature service. I certainly hope it will last longer than a week or so."

"Then you're in trouble. To get a job in France a foreigner needs a work permit. To get one, your papers must be in perfect order, including a passport with a visa."

"What happens now?"

"I'll try to find out." He turned back to the Inspector speaking French slowly so she could understand.

"Mademoiselle says she simply forgot to get a visa from the French consul in London. She is anxious to comply with all regulations because she hopes to be living and working in Paris for some time to come. Is there any way she could get a visa now in Dieppe?"

"Visas can only be obtained from French consuls abroad."

"Can't I go back to England to get a French visa?"

"No, you cannot leave France now."

"Why not?"

"You cannot leave a country until you have entered it. Officially you have not entered France."

"Then can I go on to Paris tonight?"

"No, you will have to remain here in Dieppe until the affair is arranged between your government and mine."

6

"How long will that take?"

"I haven't the slightest idea."

"Is there an American consul in Dieppe?"

"He has no jurisdiction over French visas."

Once more Sergei Radetzkoy intervened. "Just what is to become of us tonight, monsieur? After all, mademoiselle has not committed a serious crime, and I am merely the victim of a crime."

"So you say." The Inspector brooded for a moment, then shrugged. "Ah, well, if you will each give me your parole not to go beyond the city limits, I shall put you both under town arrest until this is settled."

Sergei looked at her and nodded, almost imperceptibly. She was grateful for the hint.

"Of course you have my parole," she said.

"And mine." When Sergei smiled, his blue eyes were bright as the Baltic on a sunny day.

"Now follow me." The Inspector moved towards the other end of the shed where customs and immigration officers were waiting.

Celia and Sergei fell into step behind him. She whispered, "What does town arrest mean?"

"God knows, but we'll soon find out."

2
The Pension

Night had fallen while they were going through customs. In the street outside it was too dark to see much. There was no moon, windows were blacked out and the glass in street lamps painted blue. War had turned the old Channel port into a medieval town once more.

Celia and Sergei sat in the back of a police car. The Inspector got in front beside a uniformed police driver. He had to drive so slowly that it seemed a long time before the car stopped in one of the narrower streets.

The Inspector got out. "Wait in the car while I see if Madame Grosjean will receive you."

They could just see him in the starlight, crossing the pavement to a tall, double door and pressing a bell set in a round depression like a saucer. A smaller door opened in one leaf of the double door. He stepped across a high threshold and the door closed behind him.

The driver kept his eyes on the roadway ahead and remained silent as if the seats behind him were empty.

Celia opened her lips. Before she could speak, Sergei

laid a finger across his own lips. He was right, of course. No matter how innocent you were, you didn't talk when you were under arrest and a policeman could hear you.

The Inspector came back.

"Madame Grosjean has agreed to let you stay here until your affairs are settled. You will each pay sixty francs a day half-board. This includes breakfast and dinner and a room for each of you. Now if you will please come inside. . . ."

Sergei carried Celia's suitcase and his own. They passed through the outer door into a paved courtyard. An inner door was standing ajar.

The woman on the threshold must have been a girl at the turn of the century. She still wore her skirt long, and her hair was dressed high in a coil above an impeccable pompadour, though now it was gunmetal gray.

Her hostility burned behind a transparent veil of scrupulous politeness.

"This lady and gentleman will be happier dining by themselves in the salon. My other guests are only halfway through dinner in the dining room. I see no reason to disturb them."

This was code. She was really saying: I shall protect my respectable guests by segregating these jailbirds the police are forcing upon me.

"As you please, madame," said the Inspector. "And now permit me to present Mademoiselle . . ." He glanced at Celia's passport. "Mock-neel?"

"Mock-neel?" cried Madame. "What kind of name is that?"

"Polish, perhaps. The first three letters are all consonants, *M, C, N.* How does one pronounce a name like that?"

"McNeill," said Celia.

9

"Just as I said, Mock-neel."

Madame Grosjean was looking at Sergei. "And this monsieur is . . . ?"

"Sergei Radetzkoy, at your service, madame."

She did not return his smile.

"Your rooms are on the floor above at the head of the stairs. Here are your keys. This is the salon."

She threw open a door on the right. It was a little Victorian parlor, preserved intact—Brussels carpet, plush curtains edged with ball fringe, buttoned-down upholstery, and a working fireplace where coal smoldered in an iron basket-grate.

In the center a round table had been laid with a white cloth and set for two, presumably while Celia and Sergei were waiting outside in the car.

"It looks very comfortable, madame," said Celia.

"Then perhaps we can regularize our accounts now by your paying a week in advance?"

There was a split second of shock. Celia saw a gleam bounce off Sergei's eyes like a blue spark struck from flint.

She turned to the Inspector. "Are we to be here a whole week?"

"At least that."

Celia took four hundred-franc notes and one fifty-franc note out of her handbag.

Madame started to say something about change, but Celia waived this.

"Let the extra thirty francs go towards next week's bill."

It was a small gesture, but she hoped it might establish credit and goodwill.

Sergei was not to be outdone. He handed Madame five hundred-franc notes and told her that he, too, would

10

apply the extra amount against next week's bill.

It was all in vain. Madame didn't even thank them. She made out receipts and left the room with a perfunctory "Bon appetit."

At table Celia had her first look at Sergei in a good light. He seemed younger than his twenty-three years. He was lean and brittle looking as a Russian wolfhound, but nothing else about him suggested Russia. His face was a classic oval with a slightly aquiline nose, a face that would have been at home in either England or Italy. There was probably an interesting mixture of bloodlines here.

The door opened and a small man came in bearing a platter of stew on a tray much too big for him. He was the first person to smile at them since they had stepped on French soil.

"Good evening, monsieur, 'dame. I am Charles. My wife's the cook. She's called Charlotte. Isn't that lucky? It helps people remember our names. Cider or Evian?"

They both chose cider.

"Please ring when you are ready for dessert." He was still smiling as he went out, closing the door behind him.

Sergei watched Celia taste her drink and laughed.

"You thought it was going to be hard cider?"

"I hoped it was going to be hard cider."

"This is the kind of place where you pay extra for anything like that."

"I really need a drink tonight."

"And you shall have it."

He took a flat, silver flask out of a breast pocket. It was silver and had once been handsome. Now it was dented and scratched.

"Vodka?" Celia asked.

"Heavens, no. I'm not all that Russian. My mother was

11

English, and I went to school in England. I've had jobs in France and Italy. I'm pretty much at home anywhere. This is cognac. We both need it tonight."

"Just a little for me, please."

"Oh, come off it!" He poured a healthy slug into her glass of cider, the only glass available.

After the first sip she began to feel alive again.

Dessert was a delicious cream cheese called *petit suisse*, country bread, and fresh oranges. By that time they were calling each other Celia and Sergei and she was having fun.

Then he spoiled everything.

He was looking down at an orange he was peeling when he said it.

"Did you really forget to get a visa in London?"

For a moment she was speechless. Then she rallied.

"Did anyone really steal your passport on the boat?"

"Oh, yes. That's true."

"Why would anyone steal a passport?"

"There's a black market in passports. Signatures can be forged and photos can be substituted, but they have to have authentic paper, binding, and seals."

"Why didn't they take your money?"

"They did take most of it. I was keeping the notes I gave Madame handy in a breast pocket. My wallet was in a hip pocket with my passport. The wallet's gone, too."

"And where were you while this was going on?"

"I was being sick as a dog in no condition to notice anything."

Celia remembered her own humiliating dash to the deck rail and relented.

"Why didn't you tell the Inspector all this?"

"I didn't want him to know. He would have been

12

tougher with me if he'd known I was flat broke."

"You can't be broke just because your pocket was picked."

"Oh, yes, you can. That five hundred francs I gave Madame was my last penny."

"Then why did you give it to her?"

"For the same reason I didn't want the Inspector to know I was broke. I was trying to establish credit with both of them."

"How are you going to pay next week's bill if we're still here?"

"Can't you guess?"

"No."

He looked thoughtfully at her suit. It needed pressing now, but it was a good suit—wine-red Scottish homespun, cut to measure.

"Since you are so obviously a rich American, I am going to borrow from you."

"I have news for you. I'm a poor American."

"I suppose you mean you have only five or ten thousand dollars in travelers' checks with you at the moment."

"I have no travelers' checks at all with me at the moment."

"But you have a bank account in America and—"

"I have no bank account in America, only an old account at Morgan, Harjes with no money in it. I'm just as broke as you are."

"I don't believe it. There's no such thing as a poor American."

"You'll have to believe it. All the money I have in the world is ten thousand francs cash in this handbag and I am not going to lend any of it to anybody. It has to last

13

until I get to Paris and get settled in my new job there."

"But you must have a family in America who would help you in an emergency?"

"I don't. There are just some distant cousins, very distant. They don't like me and I don't like them."

"You'll have to spend some of your ten thousand francs if the police keep us here another week."

"That's what's worrying me now. Maybe if I go to the American consul tomorrow . . . ?"

"You'll get sympathy, not money."

"Oh, dear, what will happen when my ten thousand francs runs out?"

"Ever see the inside of a French jail?"

"That's absurd."

"Not when you think about it. If we stay on here after we know we have no more money coming in to pay Madame, we're committing fraud. Either we must get the passport business settled quickly or we must get enough money to pay our bills while it's being settled."

"And if we can't do either?"

"Let's not even think about that."

"I don't suppose French jails are any worse than other jails. Such places aren't supposed to be comfortable, are they?"

"Precisely the French point of view. They call it 'Cartesian logic.' And now I'm for bed. We can resume this morbid conversation in the morning, if you're still speaking to me then."

"I probably won't be."

She regretted her flash of temper as soon as she was alone. She had taken him too seriously. His airy assumption that she would lend him money had been a piece of mischief, a tease. All she had to do was refuse him. . . .

14

She had not heard a knock, but now she saw the door of the salon was sliding open.

A head came around the corner. Eyes flicked over her. A little man nipped nimbly into the room and shut the door quickly behind him.

His style was whimsically Edwardian: cutaway coat and striped trousers with a double-breasted waistcoat of lavender-gray. A black satin stock was wrapped around his throat and held in place by a black pearl stickpin.

This foppish air was not altogether happy with a bald head, a long, inquisitive nose, and lips that protruded because they could hardly close over ill-matched jaws.

"Miss McNeill? My name is Aristides Kyros."

"How did you know my name?"

"We got it out of Charles after dinner."

" 'We'?"

"The other boarders and myself. We're all curious about you."

"Why?"

"You're a personable young woman, brought here by the police and segregated from all the rest of us with a young man. Can you wonder that we're agog? We can't get a word out of Madame Grosjean. I think she's a little afraid of the Inspector, even though he is her nephew."

"Is he?"

"Of course. Didn't you know?"

Celia shook her head. Had the Inspector brought them here because an aunt could hardly refuse her nephew a favor? Or did this aunt need the money?

Kyros pulled out Sergei's chair and sat down at the table. His right hand rested on the back of the chair for a moment and that was when Celia noticed the seal ring on his little finger.

His glance followed hers.

15

"My luck-piece."

The ring seemed a little big for him. He slid it off his finger and handed it to her across the table.

The setting was modern, an oval cartouche of plain gold. The stone was agate, desert-color, engraved with a tiny, human profile. The nose was prominent, the head crowned with plumes or flowers, she was not sure which.

"It looks old."

"Pre-Columbian. That fellow is Tezcatlipoca, the Lucifer of the meso-Americans. Only he won his rebellion. Quetzalcoatl, the Feathered Serpent, had to retreat into the sky and become the morning star."

"You're not a Mexican, are you?"

"No, I was born a Cretan. Now I am a naturalized British subject. I have a gallery in London where I sell archaic art, the kind most people call 'primitive.' I became interested in Aztecs and Incas when I saw how close some of their sculpture was to some on this side of the Atlantic. Ever see an image of an Aamand, a prehistoric Danish river troll? Pure Aztec."

Now that he had introduced himself he seemed more at ease. When she refused a cigarette he lit one for himself, narrowing his eyes against the first drift of smoke, and said quietly, "Is Sergei Radetzkoy an old friend of yours, Miss McNeill?"

"I never saw him before tonight."

"But he did come here with you?"

"We were fellow passengers on the boat. How did you know his name?"

"I thought I recognized him on the stair just now as I was coming across the hall. I've seen him on the stage several times."

"The stage?"

"Didn't you know he was an actor? Not a star, of

16

course. Just supporting parts. You'd better be careful
with him. We don't think much of him in London."

Celia rose. "Good night, Mr. Kyros."

"But you ought to know about him. He sponges off
rich Americans, especially women. That's how he picked
up all that American slang and—"

"I said good night."

Celia brushed past him and ran upstairs.

She was almost asleep when a sudden thought woke
her again.

What was the Inspector looking for when he insisted
on seeing every passport that came off the boat from
England tonight?

Wasn't it unusual to have a high-ranking police officer
take over the ordinary passport officer's job?

Who, or what, was Inspector Grosjean really looking
for on the pier tonight?

3

The Consulate

A knock on the door woke her that first morning.

"Bonjour, mademoiselle!"

Already Charles was smiling. He brought in a load of kindling and knelt on the hearthstone. No American boardinghouse would send a man into a young woman's bedroom while she was still in bed, but no American boardinghouse would have a manservant or even a working fireplace.

She felt deliciously free and cosmopolitan as she sat up in bed and watched Charles making a little pyramid of old newspapers, kindling, and coals in the grate. He opened a draft in the chimney and struck a match. Yellow flames flashed into being, whispering like taffeta. A sharp almost sweet scent filled the room. She had no idea then that, in years to come, the smell of coal smoke would become a Proustian magic carpet always taking her back to Dieppe and the lost France of 1940.

Another knock. This woman must be Charlotte, the

cook, who was Charles' wife. She was carrying a tray loaded with a pot of coffee, a jug of hot milk, a pastry croissant, and a crisp roll.

"Bonjour, mademoiselle. Fine weather, cold and bright."

"Will it last all day?"

"That I don't know. Charles and I don't have time to listen to the radio in the morning. Eighteen little breakfasts to serve all at the same hour. Think of it!"

"Is there a bathtub on this floor?"

"Past the stair, first door on the right. If mademoiselle wishes a bath she can make arrangements with Madame Grosjean."

"Arrangements?"

"The fixed price is ten francs. That includes gas to heat the water, a clean sheet to line the tub, and two clean towels. Shall I inform Madame now?"

Ten francs was only about forty cents, but Celia had no idea how long her little hoard of cash would have to last, so she said, "No, thanks. I'll wait a day or so."

Charlotte beamed. "Mademoiselle is wise. The mad English take a bath every day, but it is not healthy to abuse the privilege of the bath like that."

Celia locked herself in the bathroom and took what her mother used to call a "traveler's sponge bath." She soaped herself from head to foot, rinsed off with a wet washcloth, and rubbed down with a dry towel.

Every motion she made was mimed silently by a stranger in the pier glass against the wall. Did she really look like that? A woman's body and a child's face? What made her face so childish? The tilted nose? The short upper lip?

She ran a comb through pale, fine, unruly hair and put

19

on the homespun suit she had worn yesterday. It did need pressing now, but it was the only warm thing she had with her.

In the salon she telephoned the American consul. She was hanging up when Sergei walked into the room.

"Still mad?"

She laughed. "I never was mad. I was just trying to make you understand that my ten thousand francs has got to last me until I get to Paris, and I must get there soon. They won't hold my job open forever."

"Who's they?"

"Occidental Service."

"Never heard of them."

"A superior feature syndicate serving more than two hundred newspapers in North and South America. End quote."

"What about the American consul?"

"I just talked to him. His name is Henry Hancock and I've got an appointment with him for eleven. Would you like to come along for the ride?"

"Why not? Maybe he can tell me what I should do about my passport."

"Let's walk," said Celia.

"Isn't it too early to go now?"

"I'd like to explore the town first."

The narrow street outside the pension was still in shadow so early in the morning, but once they reached the beach front the Channel waves were dancing in the sun.

Celia looked down at the beach with dismay.

"No sand?"

"Only shingles here. Most Norman beaches are hell to walk on barefoot."

20

"Why don't Parisians go to Brittany? Lots of sand there."

"Normandy's closer. Dieppe is only a hundred miles from Paris."

"Then we could walk to Paris if we had to?"

"Let's not even think about anything so ghastly. . . ."

The American consular office was in the consul's own home, a large stone house in suburban-medieval style with sham turrets and unconvincing barbicans. Shrubs marked its boundary lines and masked its cellar windows. There were no flowers.

The consul received them in a small study at the back of the house which he used as his office. The moment Celia saw him, her heart sank. She had been dreaming of a young, practical consul who might bend a regulation or stretch a law to get a compatriot out of trouble. Henry Hancock looked old enough to have been appointed by Theodore Roosevelt or Woodrow Wilson. He had the detached, inattentive look she associated with poets or professors of philosophy. She was not surprised when he mentioned that he was writing a history of Normandy. Obviously he was left over from the spacious days of William Dean Howells when an author writing a novel or a scholar who wanted to study abroad could always enlarge his income and his acquaintance by becoming American consul in some pleasant seaport not too far from a capital. These amateurs brought style and grace to the office, and in 1940 it never occurred to them that they were doomed to vanish utterly in the new, harsh, dangerous world that Hitler would leave behind him.

His glance drifted to Sergei. "I thought you were traveling alone, Miss McNeill?"

"Mr. Radetzkoy was one of my fellow passengers on

the Channel boat. The police detained him, too, because his passport was stolen on the boat."

"Is he an American citizen?"

"No . . ." Celia hurried on. "Actually he's a Russian refugee. I mean his parents were. He has—I mean, he had—a Nansen passport. Of course he has no consul of his own so I thought maybe you could tell him the best way to get another Nansen passport."

Mr. Hancock sighed. "I can give you the address of the Nansen office in Geneva, but that's about all I can do for you, Mr. Radetzkoy."

"Thank you, sir."

"And now just what is your story, Miss McNeill?"

"I forgot to get a visa from the French consul in London before I left England to come to France. Inspector Grosjean says I can't get a visa here in Dieppe, but neither can I go back to London to get one there and I can't go on to Paris until I do get one. Just to make sure I don't, they've put me under town arrest. I have a feeling this particular situation has never arisen in Dieppe before, and without a precedent the police here don't quite know how to handle it."

"How long do you plan to stay in France?"

"A year or so probably. I'm on my way to apply for a job in the Paris office of Occidental Service. Can you think of any way I can get out of this mess?"

"I'm afraid not. If you plan to live and work in France you must have a work permit, and to get one you must have a passport in perfect order."

"But is there any law that says I have to have a visa?"

"In this situation there is only one law that counts: the accepted maxim of international law that every sovereign nation has a power inherent in its sovereignty to forbid the entrance of foreigners altogether

22

or subject to any conditions it may prescribe."

"Oh, dear!"

"Exactly. Tourists spend money and don't compete for jobs or profits or social services. But visitors who want to live and work in any country may do all those things, so it's policy to discourage them in every way possible unless there's a serious shortage of labor.

"The best I can do is to get all the particulars about your case from Inspector Grosjean and send a report to the State Department. I expect some solution can be worked out eventually, but it will take time."

"How much time?"

"Let's see." He looked at a calendar on his desk. "This is May tenth. We can hardly expect a settlement before the end of June."

"But that's nearly two months. What shall I do if I run out of cash?"

"You'll just have to cable your family in America for more money to get home. That little circular you got with your passport warned you that travelers should always carry enough money with them in travelers' checks or cash to meet any emergency. We're advised not to cash personal checks of Americans traveling abroad and we have no emergency fund to come to their relief."

Celia rose and held out her hand. "Thank you, Mr. Hancock. You've been very patient. Please let me know as soon as you hear from the State Department."

He walked to the door with them and stood there a moment looking at the low gray sky.

"Any news on the radio this morning?" he asked. "I've been too busy to listen."

"We didn't even think of listening," said Celia. "They don't have a radio for guests at the Pension Grosjean. In a way it's a relief."

23

As they walked down the street, Sergei asked, "Are you going to do what he suggested? Cable your family for fare home?"

"Didn't I tell you that my only family are some cousins who don't like me? Would you ask people who don't like you for help?"

"I'd probably put my pride in my pocket."

"My pocket isn't big enough. I might forgive them for not liking me, but I can't forgive them for not liking my mother."

"You can't just sit here until your money runs out. What about Occidental Service? Would they help you with this visa business?"

"How can I ask them when I haven't even got the job yet?"

There was a newspaper kiosk at the corner. It was Sergei who first saw the headline in *Paris Soir*.

"Calais? Why that's only eighty miles up the coast." Celia saw it then.

CALAIS, DUNKIRK BOMBED
WEHRMACHT ATTACKS HOLLAND, BELGIUM

It was Celia who discovered the small paragraph on an inside page of the *Paris Herald*.

Paris, May 10.
The Paris office of Occidental Service at 2 bis Rue de la Paix announced this morning that it will be closed for the duration of the war by order of the head office in New York. Similar orders are being sent to all Occidental's other European offices.

Their Paris correspondent, Arthur Bisset, interviewed as he boarded a plane at Le Bourget this morning, said that they had been contemplating this move for several months. He added that it is financially unrewarding to maintain the Occidental type of newspaper-magazine feature service in Europe during a shooting war. . . .

"I can't believe it," said Celia. "What am I going to do?"

She had spoken in English, but a cry of despair has the same tone in any language. The old man inside the kiosk was looking at her curiously.

Sergei pulled her arm through his.

"Let's take a walk."

"In the rain?"

"I've always wanted to see what Dieppe looks like from the end of the long mole. That's the only place I know where we can talk without any danger of being overheard."

4

The Mole

Dieppe did not look old from the water. Invasions and civil wars, plague and modern town-planning had destroyed most of the old port where Verrazano had sailed in 1524 to discover New York harbor.

Today the waterfront was dominated by modern engineering, including two big moles. In summer they would be crowded with fishermen and tourists. Now they were deserted.

It seemed a long walk to the end of the bigger mole. The farther they got from shore, the more boisterous the wind became. They leaned against it, holding onto their hats. Shore sounds died away. Soon they heard only the brisk slap of water against the mole itself and the wild, sad crying of the gulls. Beyond there was nothing but a waste of heaving, gray water.

At the very end they found a bench and sat down. When they looked back, the town had shrunk to a little cluster of houses huddled together for mutual protection. The few people on the boulevard were tiny and fantastic as figures in some Chagall landscapes.

Sergei shivered and turned up the lapels of his jacket against the wind.

"This would be a perfect place for a conspiracy," he said.

"But we're not conspirators. Just victims."

"Victims of our own stupidity. Your friend, Hancock, is probably right. You should have gone back to America and I should have stayed in London."

"Why didn't you?"

"Like you I thought I could make a fresh start in France. I was going to Paris to audition for an English part in a French play, my first chance to star, but now . . . They won't be producing many plays in the next few weeks."

"What will you do?"

"Interesting question. We've both promised the police not to leave the city limits of Dieppe. If we did leave without permission, we couldn't get far without passports or money. Especially money. You won't write home for help, and I can't because I have no home. If we run out of money, Madame Grosjean will throw us out."

"So what happens then?"

"I don't know. I was joking when I talked about jail, but, now that France is in a fighting war, we might end up in some sort of detention camp like the refugees from Spain a few years ago."

"Just because we can't pay our bills and don't have any passports?"

"They'd think up some excuse. Suspicious characters. No visible means of support. Everything always comes back to money. Is it any wonder so many people cheat, lie, steal, forge, marry, and even murder for it?"

"Sergei, what would you do now if you had all the

27

money in the world? Just stay on at the Pension Grosjean?"

"Hell, no! I'd hire a car, drive to Brittany, and bribe
some fisherman with a good boat to smuggle me into
England."

"What would you do in England? Try to find another
part in another play?"

"I might be able to do something a little more useful
than that now."

"And I might be able to get a job with some American
newspaper office in London. Would my ten thousand
francs do it?"

"Of course not. That's only four hundred dollars. If
we're going to do anything like that, we've got to get
more money."

"How?"

"There's only one way and you're not going to like it."

"What is it?"

"Lend me your ten thousand francs. I'll triple it and
get us both to England in a few days."

"By doing something illegal?"

"I'll have to break parole by going outside the city
limits, but who's going to tell the police? Nobody will
ever know about it but you and me."

"Where are you going?"

"Trouville."

"Why?"

"People play for higher stakes there."

"Are you really asking me to lend you my last penny
so you can gamble?"

"How else can you triple money in one night?"

"You're serious?"

"I was never more serious in my life."

"But suppose you lose?"

28

"I shan't lose."

"Marked cards? Double dealing?"

He laughed. "In most circles, those are fighting words, but don't worry. I'm not thinking of what cardsharps call 'sleights.' I'm thinking of skill and practice and luck."

"And one of those mathematical systems?"

"No."

"People who have systems that work never admit it, do they?"

"I wouldn't know. I don't have a system, but I have hunches. I always know when I'm going to win and I'm going to win tonight."

"I haven't said I'm going to lend you the money yet."

"You will."

"What makes you think so?"

"You're not the type to sit down and wait for a trap to close on you if there's anything you can do about it no matter how crazy that may be."

"You admit it's crazy?"

"The whole world is crazy. Why shouldn't we be crazy, too?"

Celia had heard that women were not gamblers, but now she found the possibility of making money without working or scheming strangely exhilarating. Her life had been rather dull, and adventure is always at its most enticing during a first encounter.

She had been feeling claustrophobic ever since the Inspector confiscated her passport. What better thing could she do with her money than buy freedom? Paradise itself would be prison if you were told you couldn't leave.

Sergei was watching her face.

"Well?"

She smiled. "We'll do it tonight."

"We?"

"You don't think I'm going to let you go to Trouville alone? I wouldn't miss this for anything."

"You darling!"

Quick as one of the darting gulls, he kissed her and their whole relationship changed.

5
The Casino

When they got back to the promenade, Sergei went off to see about renting a car while Celia walked back to the pension alone.

Charlotte was in the salon on her knees before the hearth, polishing brass andirons so furiously that Celia did not like to interrupt.

A sob broke from her.

"What is it?"

"Oh, mademoiselle, can you ask?"

Charlotte sat back on her heels, still clutching her polishing cloth. "They're bombing us from the North Sea to the Rhone Valley. It's on the radio. Now we'll have to go through everything we went through in 1914."

"It may not be so bad this time."

"Who knows? Charles was at Verdun. He has never been well since. *Il s'urine le sang.*"

It took Celia a moment to realize that this meant: He urinates blood.

"The doctors can do nothing," said Charlotte. "He is never really well."

"And yet he is always smiling."

"He's like that."

She threw down her polishing cloth and ran out of the room.

Celia started to follow and stopped. What could she possibly say to Charlotte now? It would be like putting a Band-Aid on a mortal wound.

Earlier in the day she had noticed notepaper in one of the pigeonholes of the salon desk. Now she sat down at the desk and pulled a sheet of the paper onto the blotter.

She hesitated for one last moment, then dipped a rusty pen into a clotted inkwell and began to write.

> Pension Grosjean,
> 23 Rue Vaucottés,
> Dieppe, Seine-Inférieure,
> France.
> May 10, 1940.

Dear Cousin Patrick . . .

Well, why not?

The family quarrel was ancient history now. It had started long ago when her father brought home a bride after the last war. The McNeills were Americanized Scots living in Boston. Mary Desmond was a lighthearted Dublin girl far too frivolous for them.

After Celia was born, her father moved his little family to France. Ostensibly he was sent there to run the Paris office of his father's law firm. Actually both sides thought separation advisable. Perhaps it was too late for separation to work. Before long there were arguments about money, and the father was charging the son with extravagance and poor judgment.

When Celia's father died in France, his mother did not answer the letter from Celia's mother. When Celia's grandfather died, no money came to Celia or her mother from his estate. The only letters came from lawyers saying that Celia's father had already wasted more than his share of the inheritance while he was living in Paris.

Celia's mother refused to ask for an accounting of the estate though her own lawyers suggested it. She took her daughter to live in London where there was a market for her pastel portraits of children. Celia grew up so alienated from her father's family that she had never even thought of writing to them when her mother died, but now . . .

She knew there was only one survivor, a second cousin about her own age, named Patrick. She had no memory of him. For all she knew he had never heard of her.

So this was rather like launching a message in a sealed bottle when you were shipwrecked, hoping that someone, anyone, would find it some day and see that it was delivered.

Dear Cousin Patrick,
    I feel it is silly to carry on a family feud when there are only two of us left. I wonder if you feel the same way?
    The bombing of northern France started last night. I am trying to get to England. If I don't make it, I suppose I'll be either here or in Paris. My address there will probably be in care of

33

Morgan, Harjes, Place Vendôme. In England you might try Morgan, Grenfell, London.

I would like to hear from you.

Yours sincerely,
Celia McNeill.

She started to cross out a word and then stopped herself. There were so many different ways of expressing the same idea that once she started picking and choosing among words she would never finish the letter.

And now how should she address the envelope?

She had no idea where Patrick was. She could not remember any family address in Boston. She would have to send her letter to the Paris office of the law firm. She remembered that address because it had once been her father's.

Patrick might not be associated with the firm now, but surely someone there would know where he was and forward a letter.

There were no stamps in the desk. Charles got her a stamp from Madame Grosjean. He offered to mail the letter for her, but she said, "No, thanks, I need a breath of air."

What she really needed was to postpone her final decision to mail the letter as long as possible. When she reached the mail box at the corner of the street, she hesitated several seconds before she dropped the letter in the slot. . . .

By the time Sergei returned to the pension the narrow street beyond the salon windows was melting in a blue dusk. He had never seemed jauntier. His smile was incandescent.

34

"All set and ready to go."

"Did you . . . ?"

He held up his hand and closed the door into the hall.

"Better keep our voices down. I'll try to answer your questions before you ask them. Yes, I found a car, at the second garage I went to. Twenty-five hundred francs for the evening. I was only a moment at the first place, so they won't remember me there."

"Isn't that a hundred dollars? Rather a lot for one evening."

"I wasn't buying an evening. I was buying discretion. I let them think a jealous husband was involved. The French will always swallow that one. I told them my identity must be a secret from everybody, including them. I gave them an intimate catalog of the lady's charms and a vivid account of her husband's brutality. By the time I got through they weren't thinking of an international driver's permit."

"Then there's only three hundred dollars left?"

"Enough for our purpose. We're picking up the car at eight. It's a good little bus, a Peugeot only three years old."

"Is it far to Trouville?"

"About sixty-five miles south as the crow flies. We'll cross the Seine at Conteville, and make it by ten."

"Didn't they even ask to see your passport?

"What do you think I'm paying them a hundred dollars for?"

It was a pity Celia had no appetite for dinner. It was especially delicious that evening—a young, broiled chicken, flavored with herbs and unsalted butter, and a freshly picked salad with a tart French dressing.

When Charles left the room, after serving coffee, Sergei leaned across the table.

35

"This is the tricky part. When Charles comes back to clear the table, say you are sleepy, wish me good night, and go upstairs to your room. Listen for Charles' steps, going to and fro in the hall between the salon and the dining room. When they stop, give it another ten minutes. Then, if the hall is empty, come downstairs quietly, put the front door on the latch, and step into the street, closing the door behind you."

"And then?"

"Turn right. You'll soon come to a small church on your left. The door's always open. Go in and sit down in the first pew on your right. I'll meet you there."

"Right, left, right," repeated Celia, memorizing. "Suppose someone discovers the front door is unlocked before we get back and locks us out?"

"They won't."

"How do you know?"

"Call it a hunch. Just put it out of your mind and trust your Uncle Sergei."

Charles came back into the room.

"Monsieur, 'dame are finished?"

Sergei rose. "Entirely finished."

Celia tried to yawn, but she couldn't.

"I'm sleepy." Her voice sounded unnatural even to herself.

Sergei took her up quickly. "Then off to bed with you. I'm going to catch the seven o'clock news on the radio. *Bonne nuit.*"

She ran upstairs. Where had she heard that *bon soir* is formal, but *bonne nuit* is intimate?

Tonight, again, there was no moon, only stars. She had to grope her way step by step through the unlighted street until she came to the little church.

36

A swarm of candle flames fluttered away from the draft when she opened the door. She slid into the first pew on her right and knelt down. Kneeling had not been part of Sergei's instructions but what else can you do in a church? And, once you are on your knees, you might as well try to pray.

It seemed a long time before she felt his light touch on her shoulder. Silently she followed him outside.

A modest car was standing at the curb, just the sort of anonymous car a lover would choose if there was a jealous husband in the offing.

By the time they crossed the bridge over the Seine, the clouds parted to show a glimmer of moon. By the time they reached Trouville, the moon had escaped the clouds altogether. In the silver light the place looked like the playground it was, all spacious lawns, orderly flower beds, and fine, sandy beaches.

They passed a building that looked like luscious French pastry.

"Isn't that the casino?" asked Celia.

"That's the public casino. In Trouville it's called the Salon. We're not going there. The heavy gambling is done at a private club called . . . guess what?"

"The Casino?"

"Naturally."

They left the car in a private parking lot.

"There used to be a man to park it for you," said Sergei. "Mobilization has changed all that."

The building was on an heroic scale. All doors were double doors. All ground-floor windows were two stories high. Pillars across the front reached from porch to roof.

"I feel small," said Celia.

"An architectural trick. Don't let it fool you."

37

They went up one side of a horseshoe stairway.

In the vestibule a little man, in old-fashioned evening dress, took three notes that Sergei handed him and gave back two cards of admission.

"I thought you said this was a club?"

"It is. The kind of club that anyone with a hundred dollars can join for the evening."

"Then we only have two hundred dollars left now?"

"That's all we need."

"What was wrong with the public casino?"

"Low stakes."

They stepped through a hallway into a lofty room. Here all the furnishings were the real thing. Only time could have so tarnished the gilding on delicate tables and chairs, or so faded the dove-gray paneling on the walls, or so blurred the classical figures woven into Aubusson carpets underfoot.

Talleyrand or Metternich would have felt at home here but for one thing: professional croupiers methodically spinning roulette wheels, shuffling cards, casting dice, and collecting or distributing counters. Somebody was making a fortune here, probably some leader of the Corsican Mafia.

Most of the croupiers were old and frail, another side effect of mobilization. That was why Celia noticed two healthy, young men moving from table to table, vigilant and ill at ease. What were they? Bodyguards? Bouncers? Some sort of unofficial police would probably be needed here.

At the cashier's desk Sergei exchanged the last of her ten thousand francs for white and gold plaques.

He turned to her, smiling.

"I see a vacant place at one of the *vingt-et-un* tables."

"Twenty-one?"

"I suppose you call it blackjack."

"I don't call it anything. I don't know the game."

The table itself was another work of eighteenth-century art, its top covered with pale, silk brocade, but the dealer would have been happy in Las Vegas. He was slim, cold, and quick as a snake.

On Sergei's right there was a tall, robust man with dark hair just beginning to turn gray. The dealer addressed him as "Monsieur le Docteur."

On Sergei's left sat an older man with yellowish white hair, flushed cheeks and round, light eyes, slightly bloodshot. He was addressed as "Monsieur le Marquis" or "Monseigneur."

Doctor and patient? Monsieur le Docteur was bursting with health and vitality. Monsieur le Marquis' hands trembled. There was always a cigarette between his lips, or in the ashtray beside him.

The player beyond him was the only woman at the table. Like the two men, she had ignored popular sentiment against evening dress in wartime. Her long, satin sheath was beautifully shaped and matched the color of her pearls exactly. Her profile was bold and sharp. It might have been cut out with a razor. Her eyes were large, dark and brilliant, set so far apart that the effect was more animal than human.

Celia found a chair a little behind Sergei where she could watch without getting in his way. She was amazed by the speed and silence of the game. The players never spoke except for their ritual cries of *un, j'y tiens, crève* and, from Sergei, the American *hit me.*

She was troubled when she realized that the game depended so largely on chance. Each player was trying to build a winning hand that would score twenty-one by discarding some cards or drawing others from the

39

dealer. The ace could count as either one or ten, face cards were all valued at ten, and other cards were scored by their pips. Everything depended on the luck of the deal and the draw. How could Sergei be sure of winning a game that had so little to do with skill?

She watched the counters at his place diminish. A little crowd had begun to gather around the table. They were all looking in his direction. Were they waiting to see him lose?

She tried to look unconcerned, but it was hard as she saw his counters dwindling steadily from eleven to eight to six.

When he had only three, she touched his wrist and whispered: "Please stop . . ."

He looked at her as blindly as a sleepwalker and pushed his last six counters forward.

The dealer began to deal once more.

Celia closed her eyes, but she could still hear the snap of the cards and the monosyllables of the players: *Crève . . . un . . .* hit me. . . .

Then came a great, soft sigh, like meadow grass stirring in a light breeze. Was it a collective sigh from the crowd around the table?

She opened her eyes.

Sergei had won.

She could not stand watching any more, but when she left the table, he didn't even look up.

She wandered into another room where she found a buffet and drank some coffee. She watched roulette, fascinated by the croupier's chant: *Faites vos jeux, messieurs, 'dames. . . . Le jeu est fait. . . . Rien ne va plus. . . .* If fate had a voice it would sound like that.

She was afraid to go back to Sergei's table, but the time came when she could not put it off any longer.

40

The crowd was larger now. The chair she had occupied was filled to overflowing by a plump woman in pink tulle. Over her bare, scented shoulder, Celia looked at the table.

She could hardly believe her eyes.

Monsieur le Docteur had five counters. Monsieur le Marquis had three. The dark woman in pearl-colored satin had one.

All the other counters were piled in front of Sergei.

6
The Road

Celia hardly knew which had been the greater shock, Sergei's losing or his winning.

When the chair near him became vacant once more, she slipped into it again.

"Chicken," he whispered without looking up.

"Sorry," she whispered back.

He did look up then and they smiled at one another.

Monsieur le Docteur glanced at Monsieur le Marquis. "I'm going to order some more counters, Clovis. Would you like some?"

"By all means."

The doctor sent one of the attendants to the cashier's desk with a check. While they were waiting, he turned to Sergei.

"Permit me to introduce myself. I am Dr. Bertrand."

The woman smiled. "Introduce us, too, while you are about it, Lucien."

"The Marquis de Varengeville and Madame la Marquise," said Bertrand.

Sergei hesitated only a moment. "And I am Marcel Dupont and this is Miss Jones."

Celia was startled. Then she understood. Word must not get back to the Dieppe police that Sergei Radetzkoy and Celia McNeill were in Trouville tonight.

Clovis de Varengeville was sorting out his new counters. The doctor was lighting a cigarette for Madame.

Celia spoke to Sergei in a low voice. "Aren't you going to stop now?"

"How can I when I've just won over two hundred thousand francs?"

"Do you mean to say you've won over eight thousand dollars?"

"Close to that."

"I should think that would be the best possible time to stop."

Sergei laughed. "There's a silly thing called sportsmanship. In French, *le sport Anglais.* It governs both sides. We can't stop because we're winning, and they can't stop because they're losing. We must abide by the rules or we'll attract too much attention."

"You've already attracted attention."

"That couldn't be helped, but I don't want to attract any more attention now."

"Then when are you going to stop?"

"When they've won back enough to satisfy honor."

"I don't believe I can stand watching you play again."

Sergei beckoned an attendant.

"Champagne at once for mademoiselle."

"I don't want a drink, thank you."

"You need one."

As if by magic a glass appeared on the table beside her.

The dealer began to cast the cards again with effortless, professional speed.

43

Sergei lost a little on the first two hands, won a little on the third.

Clovis de Varengeville sat back in his chair and looked at his wife. "My dear Ambrosine, don't you think we have had enough for one evening?"

"Certainly, if monsieur and mademoiselle will have the goodness to excuse us? We'll see you later at the villa, Lucien."

The atmosphere of the table changed with their departure. The two healthy young men Celia had noticed earlier in the evening now slid into the empty chairs. Apparently they were not bodyguards or bouncers at all. They did not introduce themselves. They concentrated on the game. One kept glancing at Sergei's hands. The other studied Celia whenever he could take his eyes away from his own cards.

Again Sergei was winning steadily. Bertrand took this with perfect good humor, but the other two were looking at Sergei with narrow eyes.

He turned to Bertrand. "It's getting a little late for us now. After all we plan to drive on to Paris tonight. Perhaps you'll take your revenge some other evening?"

"Why not?" Bertrand's voice was bland.

Sergei wasted no time on the other two. *"Bon soir, messieurs."*

They did not answer. They just sat there, watching him as he swept up his counters and turned towards the cashier's desk.

"Are you going to ask for a check?" said Celia.

"I think cash is better until we get to England. If I ask for twenty ten-thousand-franc notes, it won't be too bulky."

She looked back over her shoulder.

44

"There's no one left at our twenty-one table now, not even the dealer."

"Let's get out of here."

"Did you feel it too?"

"What?"

"Those men who joined the game after the Varengevilles left."

"What about them?"

"They were suspicious of you."

In the car he paused, one hand on the ignition key.

"Celia, I could not have done this without you. How am I going to thank you?"

"I'll be even more in your debt if you can get me to England. Have you any idea where you can pick up the road to Brest?"

"I think I can find the turn-off in a few miles if I drive towards Paris first."

"What an accomplished liar you are, Monsieur Dupont! You almost had me thinking we were on our way to Paris for a while there. What becomes of this car now?"

"I'll pay someone to drive it back to Dieppe."

The car moved forward. Celia leaned her head against the back of her seat and closed her eyes.

"Wake me when we reach Brest."

She meant it as a joke, but she was almost asleep when she was roused by a grinding screech of brakes.

Another car was blocking the way. Their own car was slewed across the road touching it. They had just come around a sharp curve. Here the road dipped into a deep hollow with pine trees on either side.

"What's wrong?"

"I don't know." Sergei's voice was colorless.

Two men were coming towards them on foot. When they stepped into the bluish glow from the headlights, Celia saw who they were, the two men who had taken the chairs left empty by the Varengevilles. This was no accident.

"You followed us?" said Sergei in French.

"*Mer-de,* no!" The younger man made two syllables of the coarse word in a voice as redolent of Marseilles as bouillabaisse.

"We heard you say you were going to Paris," said the older man. "So we went around another way to meet you here head on."

Celia's skin crawled as she saw that the younger man was holding a revolver.

"Out of the car," he said. "Both of you."

A cigarette dangled from one corner of his mouth. As he came nearer, Celia caught the thick, sweet smell of Egyptian tobacco flavored with ambergris.

Sergei got out slowly. She could see he was being careful not to make any sudden movement.

"The *garce,* too."

She did not need to be told that *garce* was an impolite word.

"Wait a minute—" began Sergei.

"Shut up."

Celia got out on her own side of the car and started walking towards Sergei.

"Stay where you are."

"What do you want?" Sergei was obviously trying to make his voice reasonable.

"The money."

"Oh, no!" Celia's cry was involuntary. They had gone through quite a lot to get that money.

46

"Like the stuff, don't you?" The younger man spat on the ground just short of her feet.

"Get on with it," said the older man. "Frisk them while I hold the gun."

The younger man looked in Sergei's wallet and saw it was full of cash.

"Now you've got the money, you can let us go," said Celia.

"Oh, no, *chouchou.*" The older man saw her wince when he used the mock endearment. She had made a mistake in letting him see her wince. Now he was sure to use the word again. "We still have a little business with you two."

"I cannot imagine any business we might have with either of you," said Sergei.

"You can't?" The older man sighed. "You don't have much imagination, do you? I can think of all kinds of business I might have with *chouchou* here, but at the moment there's just one thing I want.

"What?"

"Your system."

"What are you talking about?"

"I'm not a fool, mon ami. Don't talk to me as if I were. You could not possibly have won all that money in such a short time without a system."

"But I did."

"Don't give me that."

"Won't you consider the possibility that I might be telling the truth?"

Something in Serge's voice got through to both men. They exchanged uneasy glances. For a few seconds the little tableau of four figures and two cars was motionless in the moonlight. Then the older man

47

spoke to the younger as if they were alone together.

"You were right, Pépé," said the older man.

"I told you so, Gogo."

"I couldn't believe it. He didn't look the type."

"What are you talking about now?" asked Sergei.

"You, pal," said Pépé. "Nobody wins that much loot honestly. If you haven't got a system, you're a crook and so is she. What's the caper?"

"There is no caper," said Sergei.

"Don't lie to me."

Gogo took a step towards Sergei. The hand holding the gun rose. Was this going to be what newspapers were beginning to call pistol-whipping?

"Use the gun on her," said Pépé. "He'll talk then."

A sound came to Celia, faint, but unmistakable. It was the sound of another car approaching the curve behind them, coming from Trouville.

Gogo made a mistake. He turned his head.

Sergei grabbed the gun and the two men went down together, rolling in the road. Gogo managed to squeeze off one shot, but it went wild.

Celia snatched a stone from the road and threw it in Pépé's face. It struck his forehead. He came to a halt, shaking his head, blood seeping down one cheek.

The sound of the car was hardly any louder when it came around the curve. It was a make of luxury limousine advertised as noiseless. It had to stop when it reached the car slewed across the road.

A chauffeur got out.

Behind him, a window was lowered and a voice spoke from the back seat.

"What seems to be the matter now, Jules?"

It was the bland voice of Dr. Bertrand.

7

The Villa

Bertrand did not get out of the car. He sat serenely at the window as Jules answered him.

"Seems to be a holdup, monsieur."

Jules was dark, small, wiry, and apparently familiar with unarmed combat. One nicely calculated blow from the edge of his hand disposed of Pépé. A kick, equally shrewd, caught Gogo as he was struggling to his feet.

Celia watched with the knuckles of one hand against her teeth. "Are they dead?"

Sergei was too breathless to answer her.

"No, madame." Jules picked up the gun and smiled at her. "But they won't be going anywhere for several minutes."

"Madame" was considered a special honor when used to address a young, probably unmarried woman. That made a welcome change after *chouchou*.

"Is your car badly damaged?" asked Bertrand.

"I don't know." Sergei was brushing off his clothes.

Jules slid into the driver's seat of Sergei's car. As soon

as he turned the ignition key, the engine hummed.

"Monsieur is lucky. He is getting off with a few dents and scratches."

"I braked just before we hit," said Sergei. "Soon enough to reduce impact. Their car was standing still. They were using it as a roadblock."

"Ambush?"

"It looked that way."

"A classic situation," said Bertrand. "The big winner followed home from the game by thugs. I'm a psychiatrist, and I've always been fascinated by the tendency of criminals to repeat common behavior patterns. Are you still determined to go on to Paris tonight?"

"We must," said Sergei.

"Then at least come up to the villa with me now for a little rest before you go on. You're both in shock. It would be dangerous for either one of you to drive any distance in that state."

Celia looked doubtfully at Sergei, but he was already accepting.

"Monsieur is too amiable."

"It is nothing." Bertrand turned to Jules. "Can you push the crooks' car to the side of the road or do you need help?"

"A little car like that?" Jules laughed. "It's a knack, monsieur. Watch me."

The car was only "little" when compared with Bertrand's yacht-on-wheels, but Jules got it rolling in a minute with the same cunning application of force he had used when he planted his blows.

Bertrand turned back to Sergei. "It's only two kilometers to my villa. I'll drive my own car and you can follow in yours. Jules!"

"Monsieur?"

"Keep an eye on the situation here until the police come. I'll call them as soon as I get home. They can drop you off at the villa after they've picked up these men."

"It may take some time, monsieur. They'll want a complete statement from me."

"Take all the time you need. I won't look for you until tomorrow morning. If the police want a statement from me, they can get it when they bring you home."

"What about us?" said Sergei.

"You can leave written statements with me, if you like, and I'll pass them on to the police."

It was plain to see that Bertrand lived at the social level where the police are regarded as faithful employees rather than menacing enemies.

He drove his big car slowly and skillfully so it was easy for Sergei to follow him in the Peugeot. In a few minutes they left the road for a country lane, winding through an orchard scented with apple blossom. They could hear the giant pulse-beat of the surf, though it was too dark to see water.

In another minute the lane became a driveway leading to a large house mostly glass that glittered in the moonlight.

"Lalique?" said Sergei.

"Sort of school of Lalique," answered Bertrand. "Did you see the room he designed for the Paris Exhibition of Decorative Arts in the twenties? It stole the show. Of course I wouldn't think of buying a house like this today."

"Why not?"

"Bombs. I was in Spain a few years ago. I saw great splinters of plate glass fly through the air and slice off human heads."

Celia couldn't help wondering what Dr. Bertrand had

51

been doing in Spain then, but she didn't ask because she had a feeling he would rather not talk about it.

Inside the house there were no doors or rooms, just a series of spaces that could be closed or opened, contracted or enlarged by sliding partitions like the panels in a Japanese shoji. Light coming from hidden sources was as diffused as twilight.

Bertrand led them over a spongy carpet which silenced every footfall to a large space at the back of the house with a whole wall of glass. It was too dark outside to see anything beyond the glass clearly, but now the surf was so close it sounded like the deep purring of a lion at play. By daylight there must be a splendid airplane view all the way to the horizon.

Clovis de Varengeville was sunk deep in a modern chair slung so low that he had to make a real effort to rise.

Ambrosine stood beside a sleek, modern console table, lighting a cigarette in an ivory holder.

A disembodied voice was coming from a radio concealed in the wall, a recording of Raquel Mellor singing "Violetera."

"Our friends have had a misadventure," explained Dr. Bertrand. "Two criminal types followed them from the casino and tried to rob them on the road. Luckily Jules and I came along in the nick of time."

There was something more in Ambrosine's response than a capitalist's reflex wince at any threat to anybody's property. She stood motionless until the flame of her match had burned down to her fingers, then woke from her trance with a start and blew it out.

"Were the men identified?"

"Not yet, but they are obviously professionals. The police will know who they are."

Bertrand turned back to Celia and Sergei who were

standing a little awkwardly at the edge of the group like the outsiders they were.

"The police may want to question you eventually. If you'll just leave your Paris address with me, they can get in touch with you there."

For once Sergei was at a loss. Celia spoke quickly:

"Morgan, Harjes, Place Vendôme, will reach both of us. It's our only permanent address."

"I might have known," said Bertrand. "Isn't it the address of every American who stays in France for any length of time? And now what refreshment would you like? A little cognac? Some wine perhaps? I have a very good Côtes du Rhône here and—"

The voice of Raquel Mellor died in the middle of a bar.

Then came a high gabbling between bursts of static.

". . . four thousand paratroopers on the bridges at Rotterdam . . . Others landed at Maestricht where Belgians mistook the gliders for planes with engine trouble . . . the fortress of Eben Emael . . . Germans trying to encircle Liège as they did in 1914 . . . Winston Churchill has succeeded Neville Chamberlain . . ."

Ambrosine flew to the radio and snapped it off.

"Don't you want to hear it?" said Bertrand.

"Do we have to hear it tonight? Let us have a few more hours of peace while we can, I beg of you, Lucien."

"As you please, madame." Bertrand's voice was remote.

"And now will you kindly ring for cards?"

"Cards?" cried Clovis. "Now?"

"Have you never heard that cards were invented by soldiers during the siege of Troy?"

"I thought that was dice," said Sergei. "And it's tradition, not history."

"Does it matter?" Her scorn impaled him. "They've

53

been following both traditions all winter on the Maginot Line, and why shouldn't they? I'm glad Lucien brought you back here, monsieur, for I have a question to ask you. How do you explain your extraordinary luck at cards?"

"I cannot explain it, madame. I merely enjoy it."

She paused, as if aware of the enormity of what she was about to say, then went on implacably.

"Can it be that you sometimes assist your luck?"

Bertrand looked like an orchestra leader who hears his first violin play a sour note.

"Ambrosine, there is no question of—"

"But, my dear Lucien, I assure you that there is indeed a question of precisely that." Her splendid insolence blazed like a fire. "Can monsieur prove that there is not?"

Russians are not celebrated for even temper.

Celia could almost see the struggle going on in Sergei between his genes and his English schooling. The schooling won.

"I hardly understand you, madame."

"I think you understand me very well, monsieur, but in case you don't, I shall be more explicit. I was suspicious of your play this evening. Are you claiming that my suspicion was unjustified?"

"Of course."

"I want more than your word. I want to watch you once more while you play twenty-one. Then, if I can't find out how you do it, I'll acknowledge that you are an honest player and tell everybody that I do. We'll play without stakes, of course."

"No, madame, I never play without stakes."

"Then we'll play for whatever stakes you may care to name."

"But, Ambrosine, my dear—"

"Please do not interfere now, Clovis. It's too late. I am committed."

"My very dear Ambrosine," said Bertrand. "Aren't you losing your sense of proportion? The Germans are now—"

"Lucien, this may be the last night for years to come that we will be free to amuse ourselves as we please. Don't spoil it."

Bertrand touched a bell inlaid in the table top.

Sergei turned to Celia. "You look as if you were on your way to the guillotine," he said in a low voice.

"That's just how I feel. We ought to leave now."

"It's too late, as madame said. I've promised to play and I shall. This time I want you to play, too."

"Why?"

"Then you'll be too busy to worry."

"But I've never played this game. I don't even know when to draw or discard."

"Draw when your cards total sixteen. Odds are two to one in favor of drawing then. Stand on seventeen."

"Suppose you lose all the money you won? What will become of us then?"

"Celia, luck is a state of mind. If you talk like that, I shall lose. So don't."

A manservant came into the room. "Monsieur le Docteur rang?"

"Yes, Henri. We need a card table, cards, and counters."

"Immediately, monsieur."

There was a sly exaggeration about Henri's urbanity. He's Figaro, thought Celia. He's a comedian playing the role of a servant on an invisible stage, not a real man working at his job for pay and anxious to please. There was caricature under the surface of all his actions, when he set up the card table, when he placed chairs around it, when he laid out cards and counters.

Once they were seated, he stood at Bertrand's elbow, waiting to be noticed.

"Yes?" Bertrand spoke without looking up from the pack of cards he was opening.

Henri answered in a low voice.

Bertrand looked up, startled. "Here? Now?"

"Yes, monsieur."

"Then you'll have to show him in."

Another voice called out from the other end of the open space. "Am I intruding?"

Celia turned in amazement.

It was Aristides Kyros.

"My dear fellow, of course not."

Bertrand rose and shook hands making a ceremony of it as some Frenchman do.

"I believe you know Varengeville? And Madame la Marquise? This is my old friend, Mr. Kyros—Miss Jones, Monsieur Dupont."

"We met yesterday in Dieppe." Kyros smiled. "Only then they were Miss McNeill and Mr. Radetzkoy."

Bertrand was the first to recover. "How sensible of you not to give your real names to strangers in a casino."

"Radetzkoy?" repeated Clovis. "I used to know some Radetzkoys in Petersburg long ago."

"I've known this one for several years," said Kyros. "We saw quite a lot of each other in London, didn't we, Sergei?"

"Did we?"

"Don't tell me you've forgotten?"

"I have a bad memory for some things."

Kyros looked down at the card table. "Is this a private game? Or can anybody join in?"

"Twenty-one is not limited to eleven players like its offspring baccarat," said Bertrand.

"Is that an invitation?"

Bertrand nodded coolly.

Henri brought forward another chair and Kyros sat down at the table.

Bertrand threw a card to each player. When the cards were turned face up, Sergei had the highest card, an ace. This made him both dealer and banker.

He looked down at the counters. They were marked one hundred, five hundred, one thousand.

"Francs?" said Ambrosine.

"Naturally," said Bertrand. "After all, we are in France."

"Why don't we play for dollars?" said Ambrosine.

"Why should we?"

"It's one way of raising stakes." She smiled at Sergei for the first time. "Are you willing?"

He returned her smile with interest. "Why not have a really fast game and play for pounds?"

Celia started to protest. Sergei caught her eye and shook his head.

"Fantastic!" Ambrosine twinkled at Sergei as if she and he were sharing a delicious, private joke.

"Oh, well, why not?" said poor Clovis heroically.

"All bets shall be at the player's option within a fixed limit," announced Bertrand.

"And the limit shall be a hundred pounds," added Kyros.

Sergei performed a dextrous riffle-shuffle and presented the pack to Bertrand for cutting.

57

Before Bertrand could move a finger, Kyros leaned across the table, divided the pack into four stacks and rearranged them in a different order.

Bertrand was displeased. "I saw a man named Scarne cut cards like that in New York a few months ago. He was playing with people he did not trust."

"I trust you implicitly, Lucien," said Kyros. "I was just making this test a little more difficult for Monsieur Radetzkoy."

"But it was my turn to cut. I'm sitting on the dealer's right hand." Bertrand looked at Sergei. "Shall I ring for another pack?"

"Why bother? It will just hold things up."

"All right. We'll let it go this time, but for the rest of the evening we'll have fresh, sealed packs available whenever we want them."

Sergei dealt two cards to each player and looked at his own. Ambrosine drew one card and said: *"J'y tiens."* Clovis drew two cards, shook his head and said: *"Crève."* Celia's hand totaled seventeen, so she stood without drawing as Sergei had advised. Kyros drew three cards before he stood. Bertrand drew one and stood.

The play had now come back to Sergei. He put the two cards he had dealt himself down on the table face up, an ace and a king, the two-card winning hand that gave the word "natural" to our slang.

Kyros threw himself back in his chair. "Good God, man, how do you do it?"

"I didn't do a thing as you very well know if you were watching me."

"But you knew you had a winning hand before you picked it up. I could tell by the look in your eyes."

Ambrosine sighed luxuriously. "This is going to be exciting. I knew it would be."

58

From that moment the pile of counters at Sergei's place went on growing. In an hour he won nearly eight hundred pounds in addition to all that he had already won at the Casino.

Celia had heard that any gambler can experience an inexplicable run of luck. In France he is said to be *en veine*. In England he has "a winning streak." In America he is "hot."

Was that enough to explain what was happening to Sergei tonight?

Ever since they had set out together from Dieppe this evening, Celia had been praying that he would win.

Now she knew that she would be a great deal happier if he lost.

8

The Hollow

Gradually Celia began to realize that the sky beyond the glass wall was growing pale.

Sergei saw it, too, and turned toward her.

"We'll have to go. We're way behind schedule now.

"Oh, no!" protested Ambrosine. "You can't go now while you are still an unsolved problem."

"We've been playing for hours. Isn't that test enough?"

"No."

"Then why not go by English law and say that I am innocent unless I can be proved guilty?"

"I never assume innocence. In your case I am sure there is something peculiar going on, but I can't put my finger on it yet. Do give me a little more time. Please."

"I am sorry, madame, but that's impossible. We must be in Paris by noon."

"Oh?" This time she did not yield to anger. She took her cigarette holder out of a small bag made of seed pearls and smiled. "Have you a cigarette, monsieur?"

Her voice lingered on each word like a caress.

Out came a cigarette case, as battered as his flask. He flipped it open. "Turkish on the left, Virginia on the right."

"How English." She chose a cigarette filled with Virginia "bright" tobacco which showed yellow at either end. "These are so delicate, like China tea. We can't get them in France because of our silly state monopoly of tobacco."

Sergei flicked a match and held the flame to her cigarette. She steadied his hand with her own as she took her first inhalation, one of those little gestures that can mean everything or nothing.

Celia decided she did not like Ambrosine. At the same moment she wondered if Ambrosine and Sergei could have met before this evening?

Ambrosine leaned back in her chair and exhaled a fan of smoke. "Why don't you tell me?"

"Tell you what?"

"Your secret. I'm sure there is a secret."

Bertrand broke this up. "Ambrosine, you are becoming a bore. Monsieur Radetzkoy has been extremely patient with you, but now it is time you stopped imposing on his patience and wrote him a check." Bertrand turned back to Sergei. "You will accept checks, I suppose?"

"Of course, and there's no rush. You can mail them to me when it's convenient."

"Oh, no," said Clovis. "Such little matters should always be settled at once. I'll write a check now for both Ambrosine and myself, but my checkbook is upstairs. Please excuse me a moment while I get it."

Bertrand took his checkbook out of his breast pocket and wrote his check at the card table. He passed it over to Sergei with a smile.

"You must have coffee and rolls before you leave. People who go without sleep have to eat."

"I thought it was the other way round," said Ambrosine. "Who sleeps, dines."

"Haven't you noticed that most proverbs are reversible?" He pressed the bell inlaid on top of the console table. "I shall insist on everybody eating something. A doctor can't stand by and see the human body abused."

"I'd love coffee," said Celia. "If it isn't too much trouble."

"No trouble at all." Bertrand pressed the bell again.

"Would anybody mind if I turned on the radio now?" said Kyros.

"On the contrary, my dear fellow, I think it's time we all heard the news."

There was the usual burst of static, then a voice.

". . . General von Kleist's Armored Group crossed the minefields along the Belgian frontier last night. The First French Cavalry Brigade and the Fifth Light Cavalry Division are making a stand along the Sunois. . . ."

Kyros, writing in his checkbook now, looked up with a laugh. "Tough, isn't it? And this is just the beginning, Lucien. When this war is over, your world and mine will be dead."

"And what are you going to do then, monsieur?" demanded Ambrosine.

"Just what you are going to do, madame. Survive."

He handed his check to Sergei.

"What has happened to your ring?" said Celia.

"Ring?" repeated Kyros.

"The one you showed me last night. The little pre-Columbian god, what's-his-name, Tezcatlipoca."

Kyros looked down at his own left hand. All the fingers

were bare. "It must have slipped off. I'm underweight so it was a little loose."

"Then it must be somewhere in the house," said Bertrand.

"Not necessarily," answered Kyros. "I got out of the car once before I reached the house. I was afraid I'd run over somebody's dog, but it turned out to be a rabbit, dazzled by headlights I suppose. I could have lost the ring then. If you'll excuse me, I'll take a look along the road and see if I can spot it."

"While you're doing that we'll look in here," said Bertrand.

Kyros disappeared beyond the sliding partitions.

It didn't take long for the others to search a room furnished with such stark simplicity as this one, but there was no sign of the ring anywhere.

"What an odious, little man! Who is he, Lucien?"

"He calls himself an art dealer," said Bertrand. "Nobody seems to know very much about him."

"He was watching you all the time at the card table," Ambrosine informed Sergei. "He's just as sure as I am that you have some sort of secret."

"Ambrosine, my dear, won't you drop the subject now?" said Bertrand. "It is making everybody uncomfortable."

"Lucien, my dear, after all these years don't you realize that I enjoy making people uncomfortable, especially handsome young men?" She turned imperiously to Sergei. "We've fenced enough. Tell me now. What is your system?"

"I have none."

"I don't believe you."

"That's your privilege."

"Haven't you any explanation to give me at all?"

63

"Only one which you won't accept."

"And that is?"

"Experience, skill, and luck."

Ambrosine looked sidewise at Bertrand. "Do you believe him?"

Bertrand hesitated, then spoke quietly. "No."

Sergei's smile vanished. "Are you suggesting that I have a mathematical system?"

"No."

"Are you suggesting that I cheat?"

"Doesn't it have to be one or the other?" said Ambrosine.

"Does it?" Bertrand's eyes dwelt on Sergei. "I can think of a third explanation. Can't you?"

The thick carpet kept them from hearing Clovis' return.

Suddenly he was there with a check for Sergei.

"And now, Lucien, I'll have one last little glass of brandy, if I may."

His words were a little furry around the edges.

Bertrand was at his side instantly, a hand on his shoulder. "No, old man. You may not. As your doctor, I cannot allow it. You've had enough."

Clovis shook off the hand and smiled at Celia.

"May I come and sit by you, my dear? I like to sit by people who appreciate me. People who don't criticize me."

Ambrosine flashed a furious glance at Bertrand.

He took the cue. "Clovis, my friend . . ."

"Yes, Lucien?"

"It's daylight now. We've been up all night. You need sleep."

"But I am not in the least sleepy, my good Lucien."

"I am your doctor. I insist."

64

Clovis sighed. "I have something to tell you, Lucien."

"Yes?"

"You are no longer my doctor."

"Oh, really, Clovis!" said Ambrosine. "This exceeds everything." It was a tone she might have used to a small child.

Clovis looked at her calmly. "I have lost the old privileges of my forebears, but I have acquired some new, democratic rights in their place. One of these is the right to choose my own doctor."

"How can you be so ungrateful to Lucien?"

Clovis was looking around the open space as if something puzzled him. "Where is that Monsieur Kyros?"

"He has gone out to look for his ring."

"And where's Henri?"

"No one knows. He hasn't answered the bell."

"Then I'm going to look for him. If I can't have brandy, I want that coffee."

Clovis was gone before Ambrosine could object.

"Poor, old boy," said Bertrand. "He'll have forgotten all about this by tomorrow."

"Then why didn't you let him have some brandy?" said Ambrosine.

"It's not good for his arteries and—"

She cut him short. "Does it matter? We both know he hasn't long to live."

"As a doctor I have to say it matters."

"And what do you say as a man?"

Bertrand shrugged.

Celia thought, not for the first time, that it must be wonderful to live in a culture where you can get rid of awkward questions without saying a word.

On the other side of the glass wall, the western sky was was blushing pink before the coming of the red sun in the

65

east. There was a view of beach and Channel as Celia had guessed last night, but it was far too hazy now to see the horizon.

"Perhaps we ought not to wait for coffee," said Celia.

"I was just thinking the same thing," answered Sergei.

There was a muffled sound of feet hurrying on the thick carpet. Clovis plunged into the room.

"He's gone."

"Who?"

"Henri. He isn't anywhere in the house. I looked."

"Is Jules back?"

"I didn't see him."

"How very strange." It was the first time Celia had seen Dr. Bertrand at a loss.

"I think Henri's gone for good," said Clovis.

"Impossible. The man has been with me for fourteen years. He's absolutely devoted to me. Why should he take off now?"

"Can't you guess?" said Clovis. "The kitchen radio is still on. I think he's been listening to it all night."

"What if he has? That's no reason to take off now without giving notice or collecting wages due him. Are you sure he hasn't just stepped outside for a moment?"

"I did look out the window at the driveway. No sign of him there."

"Perhaps he's fallen asleep somewhere," said Ambrosine.

"But he's used to night duty," returned Bertrand. "He knows he'll be given time to make up his lost sleep the next day. This is out of character."

"Then why not organize a search?" suggested Sergei.

"Very well," agreed Bertrand. "You take the wine cellar. I'll take the garage. Miss McNeill can search upstairs.

66

Ambrosine can search the kitchen and pantries. That leaves the rest of the downstairs for Clovis."

It didn't take long for Celia to search the bedrooms upstairs. There were few places where a grown man could hide. As she went from one room to another she remembered her odd feeling earlier that evening that Henri was like someone acting a sly part in a comedy. Apparently she had been right. If he had been planning this disappearance then, he must have been laughing in his sleeve at all of them all evening.

Sergei was alone in the glass-walled space when Celia came downstairs again.

"No luck?"

He shook his head. "According to the kitchen radio, they're bombing Calais again. They'll be here sooner than we think."

"Is that why Henri took off?"

"Possibly. While we were gambling, he was listening to the news, so he was a jump ahead of us."

"Isn't that funny? I never wondered what he was doing when he was out of the room."

"Neither did they. They're as astonished as they would be if a piece of furniture had walked out of the house. I doubt if they ever quite realized before that he was alive."

"Are you sorry you stayed here last night?"

"I don't waste time on past mistakes," said Sergei. "I'm not even sure it was a mistake. I learned a lot of things last night I wouldn't have learned otherwise."

Before Celia could analyze this peculiar remark, Ambrosine came in carrying a beautiful, old silver tray with hot coffee steaming in white and gold Limoges cups.

67

"You remembered," said Celia. "And I forgot. I'm ashamed."

"The moment Lucien said I was to search the kitchen I knew what he had in mind. Now I must find Clovis. He's the one who first asked for coffee."

She came back a few moments later with Clovis and Bertrand.

Celia was surprised to find hot croissants and fresh butter with the coffee. She had typed Ambrosine as the idle, great lady incapable of drawing her own bath or dressing her own hair. Now she was sharply reminded that no individual human being ever fits any stereotype exactly. Ambrosine might be selfish and unkind, but she had a zest for life that saved her from being idle or stupid.

She accepted Celia's good-bys prettily enough, but Clovis was the only one of them all who sounded as if he would really like to see her again. This made her wish that she could tell him the truth that she wasn't going to Paris. She didn't mind deceiving Ambrosine or Bertrand in the circumstances, but she wished that she didn't have to deceive Clovis.

Bertrand walked to the front door with Sergei and Celia. Once more she tried to thank him for rescuing them from Gogo and Pépé, but he brushed that aside almost impatiently. It was nothing at all. He had been only too happy to help Miss McNeill and Mr. Radetzkoy out of their difficulties. Once they were all settled in Paris, they must have a reunion. He lived near the Bois in a building built on the old ramparts. They must come and see his view.

On the front steps Celia halted suddenly. "Whatever became of Kyros?"

Bertrand laughed. "If he's been listening to a radio

too, he's probably halfway to Bordeaux by now."

"Then whose car is that?"

Bertrand walked over to an extra car in the driveway that no one had noticed until then. It was an old, well-kept English sports car with the top up. He peered through a window.

"It's his all right. Those are his gloves on the front seat. Everything seems to be in order. There's even a key in the ignition."

"Maybe he's just taking a walk," said Celia. "Watching the sunrise or listening to the birds."

Bertrand smiled. "Kyros is not a country mouse. I doubt if he's ever looked at a sunrise or listened to a bird in all his life."

"Then he must still be looking for his ring," said Sergei.

"If we meet him trudging along the road, we'll bring him back to the house," added Celia.

As the car started, she looked back. Bertrand was still standing on the threshold of the open door, smiling and waving. She waved back wondering if she would ever see him again.

At the end of the driveway they passed through open gates they had not seen in the darkness last night. Had someone opened them earlier this morning, Henri or Kyros?

Sergei did not speak until they reached the apple orchard. "A remarkable man, our Dr. Bertrand."

"They were all remarkable," said Celia.

She didn't speak again until they were entering the pinewoods.

"Sergei . . ."

"Yes?"

"There's one question I want to ask you."

He sighed. "About cards, I suppose. You're getting as bad as Ambrosine."

"No. About people. Did you ever know any of them before, except Kyros?"

"You mean Bertrand or Varengeville?"

"I was thinking of Ambrosine."

He grinned. "Not guilty. I've heard of her, of course. She's considered a great beauty in Paris. But we've never met before."

"She behaved as if she'd met you before."

"She's one of those women who can establish instant intimacy if she's in the mood to do so. If she isn't, I'm sure she can be more freezing than the North Pole."

They were deep in the pinewoods now. Celia recognized the sharp curve in the road ahead. In another moment they would be in the hollow again.

"I feel as if you ought to drive faster here," she said. "It's silly, but—"

He stamped on the brake. Once again the car skidded across the road to a stop.

She would hardly have been surprised if Gogo and Pépé had stepped out of the trees again, but this time the road remained empty and wan in the predawn light.

"What's wrong?"

"I'm not quite sure. Wait here."

He got out, leaving the door open on his side of the car. The sound of his footfalls dwindled as he walked down the slope into the hollow. He stopped halfway, looking down at something in the road at his feet. From here she could not see what it was.

She listened to the ticking of the engine as it cooled.

At last she got out of the car and walked towards him. "What is it?"

"Trouble."

She tried to see beyond him.

"Don't look."

"But I've got to. You look as if you'd seen a dead man."

"I have."

He didn't try to stop her now.

Aristides Kyros was lying in the middle of the hollow. There was a wound in one temple that looked as if it had been made by a bullet. His hands lay lax upon the road, fingers half curled and bare. There was no sign of the ring engraved with the head of the god Tezcatlipoca.

Suddenly his eyes opened.

"Sergei, he's alive. . . ."

Words came from Kyros almost inaudibly.

"Look out for . . . *der rauchende Spiegel*. . . ."

His jaw dropped. Something went out of his eyes that would never come back.

A snap like the crack of a whip only louder brought her head up.

She saw Sergei's knees fold before he fell.

The whip cracked again.

A rifle?

She could never remember how she got Sergei back to the car. Years later a psychiatrist told her that blackout was a common experience under fire.

She did have a hazy recollection of the shock and outrage she felt when she found a bullet had struck one of his knee caps.

As soon as the engine turned over, she pushed the gas pedal to the floor and took the next curve in the road so fast the tires whined. Her only thought was to get away as fast as possible.

Each time she came to a crossroads she took the road that looked to her as if it would lead to a town and police.

71

She had lost all sense of direction, and signposts were confusing when you had no map. Did "Chalons" mean Chalons-sur-Marne or Chalons-sur-Saône? Could she be that far south already?

Before long she realized that she was hopelessly lost. There were no houses in sight, no other cars, no one to ask.

She drove on furiously without any idea where she was or where she was going.

Part Two

PARIS

June 1940

9

Place Vendôme

Patrick McNeill had not wanted to live in Paris. When his New York law firm offered him the Paris office, he had tried to wriggle out of it. Boston was his birthplace, New York his city of choice. Paris sounded as strange to him as Delhi or Peking.

Two years had changed all that. If he were ordered back to New York now, he knew he would be homesick for Paris. He had never really fallen in love with anybody, but now he was in love with a city.

In those days each American expatriate used to tell you that he, and he alone, had discovered the "real" Paris. Unfortunately no two of them could ever agree on where the real Paris was.

Patrick's "real" Paris was the Sorbonne neighborhood, called the Latin Quarter because medieval students had spoken their only common language there.

The Place du Panthéon was not what Patrick's mother would have called a good address. His rooms were students' quarters, large but old and shabby. There was no

75

elevator in the building, no refrigerator in the kitchen, and the cast-iron radiators remained ice cold all winter because, as the concierge said, they would not "march."

Patrick was new to French idiom then, but he soon learned that "march" is a word-of-all-work, meaning go and walk and run and work and all sorts of other things besides march.

There were many compensations for the cold. He was perched on top of the highest hill on the Left Bank, where Sainte Geneviève had once begged Attila to spare the city. He had a wide view of the sky and the Place and the library and the law school. He had real fireplaces in every room, burning real wood that was incredibly cheap. He could have mulled wine and buttered rum and roast chestnuts any evening snow blanched the dome of the Panthéon in the moonlight.

The barracks of the Garde Republicaine were somewhere over the hill. Dropping off to sleep, late at night, he would often hear the clip-clop of their horses' hooves on the cobblestones and dream that he was living in d'Artagnan's Paris.

Who wants radiators that "march" anyway?

On the morning of June thirteenth, Patrick followed his usual routine: a hot bath, a cold shower, and a glass of orange juice, a breakfast drink still uncommon in the France of 1940.

As he dressed, he listened to the radio.

The Paris station had a new call signal taken from the "Marseillaise." The newscast itself was less martial. The new head of the city's military government, General Dentz, had just announced that every step was being taken to ensure the safety and provisioning of the inhabitants.

Patrick was stunned. Only yesterday there had still been hope.

Still shaken he stepped out of his building's shadowy vestibule into the sunlit stillness of the Place. An open city? It looked more like a closed city. All the shops on the Rue Soufflot that had iron shutters had drawn them down. All doors and windows were shut. The only other human beings in sight were the policeman on sentry duty in front of the *Mairie* or town hall of the Fifth Arrondissement and the old newspaper vendor in the kiosk at the corner.

Both knew him. The policeman saluted. The news vendor rolled up the three newspapers Patrick bought from him every morning, French, English, American.

As he crossed the empty, cobblestoned Place he felt as conspicuous as an actor alone on a stage. Would the little creamery, overshadowed by the law school, where you could get eggs and bread as well as milk and cream for breakfast, still be open?

It was.

Madame the proprietress smiled as she brought his usual breakfast, milky coffee, one roll, one pat of unsalted butter, one egg "in the manner of the cock," and what a sexy way that was to decribe anything as innocent as a boiled egg.

All this for five francs, twenty cents American money.

There were no other customers, so madame lingered by his table, polishing its marble top with a cloth.

"I was afraid you might not be here this morning," he said. "Do you plan to stick it out?"

"But, of course, m'sieu. Everything I have is here."

"The papers say they may be here in twenty-four hours."

77

"I have no other place to go, and then . . ." She laughed. "War is very interesting in Paris."

He liked the implication that war might be rather a bore anywhere else.

He had heard the spot news on the radio, so he skipped the headline stories now and turned to smaller items. That was how he came across a little paragraph on an inside page of the *Paris Herald.*

AMERICAN GIRL STILL MISSING
Dieppe, June 13 Agence Havas.
There is still no trace of Miss Celia McNeill, the American visitor to Dieppe, who disappeared here over a month ago. Inspector Grosjean, who is handling the case, would welcome information from anyone who has seen her or who knows anything about her whereabouts at the present time.

It is always a shock to see your own name in print unexpectedly. This McNeill was spelled like his, not Mac-Neill or McNeil. Weren't there some cousins on his father's side who lived abroad? Could one of them be named Celia?

His glance went on to a small picture of a smiling girl that looked like a passport photo. Celia McNeill, said the caption. Has anyone seen this girl?

The picture was so smudged that he would never be able to recognize her feature by feature, but he thought he might recognize that smile anywhere.

It came to him that a month was a long time to be lost, and, with a German army in Normandy, no one there would have much time to look for her now.

Usually he walked to his office, but this morning the

idea of going alone through such empty streets was depressing, so he boarded an S bus.

The only other passenger standing on the back platform in the fresh air was an elderly man with the red ribbon of the Legion of Honor in his buttonhole. The Latin Quarter was full of men who had been decorated, mostly professors.

They didn't speak, but they exchanged bows and smiles when the old man got off, the smiles of two strangers who happen to share the same lifeboat for a little while.

Patrick left the bus near Concorde and walked up the Rue Castiglione to his office in the Place Vendôme.

It was there that he noticed the girl.

She was just ahead of him, walking slowly as if she didn't really want to go where she was going.

Most women who trekked across the wide Place so early in the morning were going to the bank, and they were usually overfed, overdressed, and over fifty. This one was young, and looked as if she hadn't been getting enough to eat. Her white, cotton voile dress and wide, black crinoline hat were hardly haute couture, but hair of a lovely, amber shade shone through the hat's transparent black crown, and this made Patrick long to see her face.

She didn't look at Napoleon's column like a tourist. She passed the Ritz and Morgan, Harjes without a glance, but when she came to the entrance of his own office building, at the corner of the Rue de la Paix, she stepped into the vestibule.

He followed and found her questioning the concierge.

"Monsieur McNeill? Second floor."

"Are you looking for me?" he asked in English.

79

She turned swiftly. The fair hair had not prepared him for dark eyes, nor had he expected such a look of anxiety.

"I'm Patrick McNeill." He had hoped his name might put her at ease, but it had just the opposite effect.

"You can't be."

"Why not?" He was smiling, but she had no answering smile for him.

"I thought you would be older. I would never have come here if I'd known you were so young."

"I'm not all that young." He was still trying to reassure her. "Why don't we go up to my office?"

There was no elevator, but the steps were shallow and they had only two flights to climb. He took her past the receptionist into his private office and placed an armchair for her facing the windows, but she was just as indifferent to his view of the Place Vendôme as she had been to the Place itself a moment ago. This piqued him, for he was rather proud of that view, but he still tried to make his voice friendly and encouraging as he went on:

"Tell me what I can do for you."

"I don't know." Her voice was desolate. "Nothing, I suppose. I ought not to have come here."

He laughed. "Does the mere sight of me convince you that I am both immature and incompetent? That doesn't augur well for my future as a lawyer."

This little attempt to divert her didn't even gain her attention, so he spoke more brusquely.

"You haven't told me your name yet."

"Celia McNeill. Does that mean anything to you?"

For a moment he thought he had discovered the cause of her anxiety.

"Of course. You're the cousin I've never seen. Some forgotten family quarrel." He put extra warmth

80

into his smile now. "I'm glad you looked me up. I've always wanted to belong to a big, clannish family, but I don't have any brothers or sisters and you're my only cousin."

She tried to smile, but he could see she was trying. So it wasn't worry about the old quarrel that made her hesitate to confide in him now. This was some newer, sharper source of distress.

"Did you come here to consult me as a lawyer?"

"Oh, no . . . " Her eyes fled before his as if she couldn't bear to look at him. "You didn't get a letter from me, did you?"

"No, was it important?"

"It isn't now. I wrote it from Dieppe over a month ago. Everything's changed since then."

"So you are the Celia McNeill who disappeared in Dieppe?"

"Disappeared?"

"There was an item about you in the *Paris Herald* this morning. An Inspector Grosjean is looking for you. Shall I let him know you're here?"

"Oh, no, whatever else you do, don't do that."

"Celia . . ." The name slipped easily from his tongue as if he had known her all his life. "Don't you think you'd better confide in me? Isn't that the reason you came here today? Why are you holding back now?"

She paused, and he suspected she was choosing her next words carefully. "There's nothing to confide except a series of misadventures. They're all over. I'm safe in Paris now."

"Safe? In the middle of an invasion?"

"I mean as safe as anybody else who's here."

"But what is this all about? I'd like to help if I can."

"Thanks, but I don't need help any more. It's over."

"What's over?"

"All right, I'll tell you, but it's quite a long story."

"I'm listening. I've got all morning."

Once she was launched on her story he had a chance to observe her more closely. Fatigue he could understand, but why the anxiety now that she had reached Paris and found him? And why did her eyes keep coming back to the clock on his desk as if she were afraid of something that might happen too soon or too late?

When she first mentioned Bertrand he interrupted her.

"Dr. Lucien Bertrand? The psychiatrist?"

"Yes. You know him?"

"All Paris knows him or knows of him. I don't know him personally."

She was speaking more rapidly now. He had a feeling she was hurrying to the end of her story now and leaving out a good many details.

"When Sergei and I left the villa, Kyros was the only one who wasn't there. A mile or so down the road we found him. He had been shot."

"Had you heard the sound of a shot before you left the house?"

"We couldn't have heard one inside that modern house. It's soundproofed."

"Was he dead?"

"Dying. Just before he died he said something strange, partly in English and partly in German. He told us to look out for *der rauchende Spiegel,* the smoking mirror. Then just after he died someone began shooting at us. Someone we couldn't see. Sergei was hit in the knee. I got him as far as the car, but when I drove on I got lost.

"From then on it was nightmare. I found at last that I was driving towards the war instead of away from it. We could see the flash of artillery on the horizon and hear the blast that comes so long after the flash. That pause between flash and blast is the longest pause in the world. Until you hear the blast you don't know how close it's going to be. But you know it's already happened. It's already past, not future, and so it's inescapable.

"We ran out of gas. Luckily, perhaps. For just after we left the car it was bombed and everything in it was burned, including our suitcases. We took shelter in the cellar of a bombed-out farmhouse. We were there several weeks, scrounging what food we could get, some of it rotten fruit that made us sick, but what else could we do? Sergei couldn't walk. His wound was infected and he developed a fever."

"You were lucky to get out at all," said Patrick. "How did it happen?"

"The fighting edge of the war passed over us and rolled on towards the coast. A stranger, who had managed to get hold of some gas for his old, battered car, gave us a lift to Paris and . . . here I am."

"You must have a remarkable guardian angel," said Patrick. "Even your clothes don't look as if you'd been hiding in a bombed-out farm house."

"I was lucky there," said Celia. "I had a small overnight bag with me when the car was bombed. This summer dress and hat were in it. That's probably one reason the police didn't find me. The description of me they sent out must have said: 'Last seen wearing a wine-red wool suit and hat to match.'"

The word police brought Patrick back to serious business again.

"Is it possible that Kyros was shot by one of the people at the villa that night?"

"I can't imagine any of them doing a thing like that."

"I didn't mean psychologically possible. I meant physically possible. Anything is psychologically possible."

"Oh, no!"

"Oh, yes! You say the last time you saw Kyros alive he left the room to look for his ring. Some time later the rest of you were separated. Was any one of the others alone long enough to have shot him?"

"I suppose so, but I still can't believe that anyone there would have done such a thing."

"Were there any other servants besides Jules?"

She hesitated. "No."

Why had she hesitated? Was she protecting somebody?

He put down his pen and looked at her.

"What else happened?"

She smiled. "Isn't that enough?"

"Is it? You were lucky. You got away. You're alive. So what is it you're so afraid of now?"

"I'm not afraid now."

Lawyers develop an instinct for truth in a witness. All that she had said might be true, but he was sure that it was not the whole truth.

"Ever since I spoke to you downstairs, you've been anxious about something," he said. "Didn't you come here because you were afraid and thought I could help you?"

"No. There's no way you can help me. And now I must go." She rose.

He rose more slowly. "I'd hate to lose a new cousin when I've only just rediscovered her. Where are you staying?"

"At the Hôtel de l'Université, in the Rue de l'Université."

"So you're on the Left Bank, too, and not far from me.

84

I live on the Place du Panthéon. Why don't you and Radetzkoy dine with me this evening? How about the Union Interalliée around six? It's just across the river in the Faubourg Saint Honoré near the British Embassy. We can have dinner in the garden if the weather holds."

She looked at him and for a moment there was more sadness than anxiety in her look. Then she managed another smile.

"Thank you. I'd like that and so would Sergei."

Was it going to be that easy? Something told him that it wasn't.

He went out into the hall with her and gave her goodbye at the front door.

Back in his own office, he sat on a window sill and watched people in the Place below passing in and out of the Ritz during the lunch hour. There were a few more than usual, for the Ritz had acknowledged the existence of the war by closing its other entrance on the Rue Cambon. Just how this would help the war effort, Patrick had been unable to discover, but it did create a feeling of crisis in patrons on the Cambon side, who had to walk several extra yards around to the Vendôme side to get into the bar.

There was a tap on the door and the head clerk, old Charley Snyder, walked into the room. Old Charley was a veteran of the last war, who had married a French girl and settled down in Paris afterward. He knew the city better than anyone else in the office, and he was trusted with secrets the partners would not have shared with anyone else.

He put down the sheaf of cardboard files he was carrying on Patrick's desk.

"Shall I destroy these now?"

"Destroy them? Why?"

"There are some things it would be just as well not to have around if we should receive any visits from the Gestapo in a week or so."

"I suppose you're right, but it's all so melodramatic I can't quite believe in it yet. What have you got there?"

"Item, a case that involved an investigation of industrial sabotage in Germany. The record includes the names of people working against Hitler there. Item, a series of letters to one of the partners from his old professor of international law at Heidelberg whose references to his Führer are irreverent. Item—"

"That's enough. Burn them all and flush the ashes down the drain. Anything else?"

"Here's a letter that came for you this morning. Apparently it's been lying around some Norman post office for weeks."

Patrick saw the Dieppois postmark as he opened the letter, so he was prepared for Celia's signature.

He read it slowly, weighing every word. One line touched him because it said so much and so little.

I would like to hear from you. . . .

Then why had she been so reticent when they finally met? What had really really happened to her since she wrote that letter?

He looked up and saw old Charley Snyder still standing there.

"What do you know about Dr. Lucien Bertrand?"

"He's a psychiatrist from northern France who started practice in Paris in the thirties."

"Successful?"

"Very."

"What about the Marquis de Varengeville and his wife?"

86

"He comes from one of those old families that goes back to the Garden of Eden. The founder of his family probably owned the land where that apple tree grew. She was a Mademoiselle Ambrosine Draguet. The founder of her family was a Swiss watchmaker to Louis XVI. In one of Balzac's novels there's a character who shows off by flaunting 'one of the prettiest little watches that ever came from Draguet's workshop.' Her grandfather switched to planes before 1914 and made a fortune."

"Charley, you're just an old gossip. You're not telling me what these people are. You're just telling me where they came from."

"That's all I know."

"Then see if you can find out something more."

When Patrick was alone, he reached for a Paris telephone book and looked up the number of the Hôtel de l'Université.

"Madmoiselle Celia McNeill? There is no one of that name registered here, m'sieu."

"Have you a Monsieur Sergei Radetzkoy?"

"We do not have him either. I am sorry. . . ."

Had they registered under false names? Surely she would have told him if they had.

He waited an hour at the Union Interaliée. Then, when he was sure she wasn't coming, he looked in the Paris telephone book again, this time under the letter *B*.

"Dr. Bertrand? . . . I am Patrick McNeill, a cousin of Miss Celia McNeill, whom I think you know. I'm anxious about her. Would it be possible for me to see you this evening?"

"Anxious? I'm sorry to hear that. If I can help, I shall be glad to do so. I'll be at home here all evening."

"Then I'll be with you in a few minutes. Thanks."

*   *   *

87

Celia left autobus S at the head of the Rue Soufflot and crossed a corner of the Place du Panthéon to the Rue Clotaire. It was a short street leading into the Place de l'Estrapade, not a real *place,* just a small, irregular open space where three streets converged. At its center four spindly plane trees were struggling to suck life from the polluted city earth.

When Celia had first come there, she had asked what the word *estrapade* meant, only to find that it was a French translation of the Spanish word *strappado* which meant a device for hanging people several times over without quite killing them the first few times. The gallows and the dark, little medieval houses where people had watched this from their windows had been gone for centuries, but the name of the Place was a reminder that in Paris, as in Scotland, the past is so close that you feel as if you must catch a glimpse of it whisking out of sight around the corner if you look quickly enough.

Today butter-colored sunlight was filtering through the tender, green leaves of early summer, and the nineteenth-century houses seemed to doze in its warmth.

Celia rang a bell at the third house she came to. The door made a clicking sound and opened. She walked past the concierge who had worked the mechanism, an old woman absorbed by her knitting who sat in a little cubbyhole under the stair.

There was no elevator, just this steep, spiral staircase, lighted by a small window on each landing.

On the fourth landing, Celia rang another bell.

The door opened instantly.

Henri stood there in his shirt-sleeves, unshaven, scowling. He pulled her into the room by one arm, and slammed the door.

88

"Where is he? This rich cousin of yours?"

"I don't know where he is now."

"Why didn't you bring him back with you? That's what I told you to do."

"I couldn't."

"Why not?"

"I liked him. I couldn't bring him back to this . . . trap."

"You'll just have to think of some other way to get him here now. How are you going to do that? Any ideas? You'd better think quick or it will be the worse for your crippled Russian friend."

"I can't."

"Oh, yes, you can."

He struck the side of her head so hard that she staggered.

10

Les Ramparts

Patrick had heard that things which happen to you do not seem real unless other people know about them. This might be one cause of indiscretion. You told other people things you should have kept to yourself because you had to make them real. Without that you would not be able to absorb them.

He must watch this temptation while talking to Dr. Bertrand. He was going there to get information about Celia, not to give it away.

It was a long drive from the Faubourg Saint Honoré to the old ramparts, but the taxi driver said he knew the route well. In the twenties he used to drive René Lacoste out there from the Stade Roland Garros to his apartment overlooking the Bois.

The only trace of the old ramparts now were a few grassy mounds where daisies grew, but they had been a Maginot Line in 1871, a wall and bastions placed at exactly a cannonball's distance from the edge of the city.

Today the place was still more country than city or

suburb. No shops in sight. Just a plantation of trees in full, green leaf and a row of tall apartment houses as uncompromisingly modern as Celia's description of the Norman villa where Dr. Bertrand had taken her and Sergei. Was the doctor a man who had no feeling for the past?

His apartment was the only one on the top floor of his building. There was a roof terrace on all four sides planted with vines and flowering trees that did something to soften the harsh lines of the concrete box that housed the dwelling.

The man who opened the door was small, dark, and wiry with eyes that missed nothing.

"Monsieur McNeill? This way, if you please."

They passed through large rooms, plush with thick carpets and deeply cushioned chairs, all in subdued colors to set off the blaze of Matisses and Chagalls on the walls. They passed through glass doors to a terrace looking towards Paris.

The light was fading rapidly, but there was still a pale vision of Sacré Coeur and the Eiffel Tower in the distance looking unreal as a dream or a memory. Some Parisians deplored the architecture of both, but to Patrick they were symbols and therefore beyond criticism.

Dr. Bertrand was dressed for a summer evening in the suburbs, short-sleeved shirt, linen slacks, rope-soled espadrilles, and a silk scarf loose around his throat. He had a young man's figure, and in a dimly lighted salon he might have passed for thirty, but in this merciless, outdoor light he looked at least forty.

In that first, quick impression of him Patrick concluded that this was a man of many experiences, not all of them pleasant. But Bertrand's smile, voice, and manner were

91

so engaging that after five minutes with him you forgot all that.

He was standing with his back to the view, his hands resting on the railing behind him. He stood erect as soon as he saw Patrick, pushing himself away from the railing.

"It is good of you to see me at such short notice," said Patrick in French.

"But it's the least I can do in your circumstances," Bertrand answered in English.

Patrick had been in Paris long enough to learn that when two people speak two languages each may have a scarcely conscious desire to show off his proficiency in the other's tongue. So the polite thing is to speak your own tongue if there is any hope of being understood at all.

Bertrand proved fluent and easy in English.

He was delighted to see Mr. McNeill. . . . Yes, it was an unusual view of Paris. . . . Cognac, perhaps? Jules could procure it instantly. . . . Do sit down. . . . A cigarette? No? . . . How wise to give up smoking. If only he could break that vile habit himself. . . .

Patrick answered in monosyllables waiting for the record to run down. At last it did.

Bertrand lit another cigarette and spoke in quite a different voice. Was it more wary? Or just more serious?

"On the telephone, I gathered that you want information about your cousin, Miss McNeill, and her friend, Mr. Radetzkoy."

"Yes. I saw my cousin today for the first time. She was supposed to meet me for dinner this evening with Radetzkoy, but they never appeared. I'm worried about her.

"She told me she was at the Hôtel de l'Université, but, when I telephoned, they said she wasn't there."

"Has your cousin any reason to avoid you?"

92

"None that I know of, and she didn't behave that way when we were together, but . . ."

"But what?"

"She did behave as if she were anxious about something. Have you any idea where she could possibly be now?"

"Alas, no. The first I knew that anything had gone wrong was when the body of Aristides Kyros was found on the road near my villa.

"Celia told me about that. She and Radetzkoy found him."

"Then why didn't she and Radetzkoy report his murder to the police?"

"Some sniper began shooting at them. Perhaps he didn't want the body found so soon. They had to run and Radetzkoy was wounded. They got lost on unfamiliar roads and only reached Paris yesterday."

"You realize that all this must be reported to the police in both Paris and Dieppe now?"

"Of course. After all I am a lawyer. Have these two crooks, Pépé and Gogo, come to trial yet?"

"No." Bertrand answered with a trace of embarrassment. "As a matter of fact, I've just had word from Normandy that they have managed to escape."

Patrick came to his rescue. "These are not normal times. The police must have a lot of other things to think about now."

"Thanks for saying that, but there's really no excuse." Bertrand sighed with vexation. Then, without warning, he attacked. "Has it occurred to you that your cousin may know more about all this than she has cared to admit?"

"She's not the kind to get involved in crime."

"But what about Radetzkoy? She's involved with him

93

and he may easily be the kind to get involved in crime."

Patrick felt the way a horse must feel when it is checked with a curb bit. All his life he had assumed that the legal way out of any dilemma was the only decent way out for a sensible person. Now, against his will, he was being forced to consider the possibility that, in this case, the legal way out might endanger Celia.

His legal training was telling him that he must go to the police even if it did endanger her, but his heart was telling him to wait and find out more about the situation before he took an irrevocable step.

"What do you know about Radetzkoy?" he demanded.

"Very little. I made some inquiries when I got back to Paris. The family comes from the Baltic coast of Russia, and they have ties with Sweden and Livonia. Sergei's father was a professor of mathematics at the University of Moscow, who became a member of the Duma. He voted for the liberal government of Prince Lvov in 1917. Sergei himself is half English. His mother was one those many, young English governesses who lived with Russian families before the revolution. She married her employer's eldest son.

"They got out of Russia in 1918 with hardly any assets. They lived in Paris and Rome because living was cheaper on the Continent in those days, but they managed to send their only son to school in England. They were disappointed when he went on the stage.

"As you see, I could not learn anything about him that accounts in any way for his extraordinary luck at cards."

"Was it luck?"

"An interesting question."

"Well?"

"If you are as poor as he has been most of his life, it must be quite a temptation to cheat. On the other hand,

I did watch him carefully at the villa that night, and I saw no evidence of cheating."

"What about a mathematical system? You said his father was a professor of mathematics."

"I suppose it's possible, but nothing he said or did while he was playing suggested it."

Patrick smiled. "You'd hardly expect a successful card-sharp to betray himself to anybody watching him, would you?"

"I'm not anybody," returned Bertrand. "I'm a psychiatrist as you probably know. When my patients go into free association they come up with a great deal of curious information. Some of them are cabinet officers, and that's why I shan't leave Paris until tomorrow. I have files to burn tonight. Two of my patients have been card-sharps so I was able to watch Radetzkoy with an educated eye. I didn't see any of the usual signs of cheating."

"What are the usual signs?"

"The crudest are trick shuffling and marked cards. The most subtle is a confederate who watches the drift of the game and signals you the right moment to raise your bets."

"What do you mean by drift?"

"In twenty-one high or low cards seem to come into play in a series of sets. Don't ask me why. I'm not a mathematician, but I've been told that fortunes have been made by using drift as a guide to betting, and casinos are on the watch for it. They bribe such players to stay away. So far as I can tell, Radetzkoy does not fit any of these patterns, which makes him a rather fascinating puzzle."

"Then, all things considered, it was stupid of Radetzkoy to make himself so conspicuous by winning at cards at the Casino that night?"

"Stupid? That's one way of putting it. I don't think he had much choice. Remember Jean Valjean in *Les Misérables*? The only way he could rescue a man being crushed to death by a wagon wheel was by displaying his unique physical strength before the police. He knew the police would identify him by that strength and arrest him, but he did it.

"The only way Radetzkoy could get enough money to get your cousin out of France before the Germans arrived was to display his notorious luck at cards in a casino. I think he knew it would get him into trouble, but he did it. I can only conclude that he must be in love with Mademoiselle Celia."

Patrick found this idea so distasteful that he changed the subject quickly.

"Did you encourage Radetzkoy to play cards at the villa because he was a riddle you wanted to solve?"

"Of course. I asked Ambrosine de Varengeville to challenge him so he would have to play. She was only too delighted to do so."

"Then you and she created the situation that led to the killing of Kyros and the wounding of Radetzkoy?"

"Neither Madame de Varengeville nor I could possibly have anticipated that. I doubt if it was cause and effect."

Patrick didn't want to antagonize Bertrand. He needed his help. So he went back to Celia.

"Have you any notion where Celia is now?" he said. "Can you suggest anything I can do to find her?"

Bertrand shook his head.

"Then I'd better get on to the police right away."

"Do you really think you can interest them in the disappearance of one girl only a few hours before the Germans enter the city?"

"I can try. Where do I go? The Préfecture or the

Sûreté? Can you give me a name to ask for? I have no police contacts. I'm not a criminal lawyer."

"I can do better than that. I can send you to Clovis de Varengeville. He knows everybody in Paris. He is even close to Paul Reynaud. If anyone can help you, it is he."

"Where can I find him?"

"He lives in the Rue de Bellechasse near the Lyceum Club. Did you dismiss your taxi? Then Jules can drive you there and I will telephone Clovis that you are on your way so he will be ready for you."

In the living room, Bertrand switched on the light and rang for Jules.

"Do you know German?" asked Patrick suddenly.

"I studied in Vienna. One of my teachers was Freud himself."

"Then you must know German quite idiomatically. Have you ever heard the phrase *der rauchende Spiegel*?"

Bertrand pondered this aloud. *"Le miroir qui fume*
. . . the smoking mirror . . ."

"Have you any idea what it means? Is it folklore or slang? Could it be code?"

"I don't know," said Bertrand. "I never heard it before."

But there was a blankness in his eyes that told Patrick more clearly than any words could that Bertrand was lying.

11
Faubourg Saint Germain

Jules knew the way. He had obviously taken this route from the old ramparts to the Faubourg many times before.

He brought the car smoothly to a halt between the boulevard and the river, then hopped out to open the door of the car and ring the bell at the Hôtel de Varengeville.

"Take all the time you like, m'sieu. I'll wait for you."

"Thanks."

Patrick was so preoccupied with his own thoughts he hardly knew what he was thanking Jules for.

The tall, double doors here were not unlike those on some of the small hotels and pensions, but the majordomo who opened one leaf of the door would never have been found in a pension. He bowed without a hint of smile and murmured, "Monsieur McNeill? This way, if you please, m'sieu."

The courtyard was a cobblestoned space surrounded by a few flowerbeds. In the middle, a large moving van was parked, and several men in shirt-sleeves were loading it with wooden crates, some cubical, like chests, others flat and square or oblong as if they contained pictures. They were all heavy, and the men, working with frantic haste, were shouting instructions to one another in the uninhibited language of soldiers.

Patrick followed his guide through another door into a square hall and up a stair with easy shallow steps designed for eighteenth-century seigneurs who had taken too much wine. In the upper hall the man opened another door and announced sonorously:

"Monsieur McNeill."

The light that came from lamps and sconces in that room had a faint tinge of aquamarine, a reflection of walls lined with faded applegreen paneling. Old paneling was usually painted cream or fawn or gray, but every now and then you came across this slightly faded applegreen, by far the most charming background for the soft shades of overdoor paintings by Boucher or Fragonard and the muted colors of antique Aubusson underfoot.

The room was all of a piece, its scrolls and acanthus leaves of the same period, in the same spirit. It was as whole and as exquisitely preserved in every tiny, fragile detail as the legs and wings of a fly frozen forever in amber. Patrick had something of the feeling of an archaeologist coming across something so old and fragile that he fears it may crumble to dust at the first gleam of daylight or the first breath of fresh air.

There were three people in the room at the moment, but none of them were betraying the unseemly anxiety of the packers in the courtyard below.

The woman with the bold face and jet hair must be Ambrosine de Varengeville. Tonight she was wearing the little, black dress of the twenties that had never gone

99

out of style in Paris. When so many women went into mourning after the first war, the haute couture made an historic discovery. Now that it was socially acceptable to paint eyes and lips, black was suddenly becoming to most women and nothing set off an artfully painted face and handsome jewels so effectively.

When short skirts and light stockings were added to draw attention to the legs, and nails were painted to match the lips, the result was so irresistible that it became a uniform rather than a fashion.

At the moment Ambrosine was in shadow where her dress and hair were scarcely visible, but the rest of her was all the more noticeable. Eye shadow enlarged and brightened eyes already large and bright. Powder gave her face a pale, velvety surface. Smoke-colored stockings and high-heeled sandals emphasized shapely legs and feet. She had the taste to use jewels sparingly—a diamond and emerald clip at one side of the high, round neck, and a large, square emerald that flashed like an exploding star whenever she moved her right hand.

It was almost as easy to identify Clovis. The stout body, too well fed for a man his age, and the pale, protruding eyes with their amiable expression were all very much as Celia had described them.

It was the other man who puzzled Patrick. He was young enough to be a student, large and shy and awkward as a puppy who has not yet got used to the length of his own legs or the clumsiness of his own reflexes. His hair was a bleached yellow; his eyes like skimmed milk, bluish rather than blue. He had a winning smile when he forgot himself, but he didn't forget himself often. He was working hard at being agreeable, as if he were trying to follow some manual of correct behavior that he had not had time to memorize.

He was introduced by Ambrosine quite simply as "Monsieur Konrad." His French was fluent, but it wasn't French French. He didn't make mistakes in grammar or pronunciation, but he had the wrong cadence. The French do not really speak in sentences. They speak in smaller clusters of words, their voices rising and falling rhythmically with each cluster. This has been called "speaking in garlands."

But Monsieur Konrad spoke in sentences. Could this be foreign French? Polish or Austrian? Then why did the buttons on his blazer show the little horse's heads of the Jockey Club? After a moment Patrick remembered hearing that the president of a Central European jockey club may be an honorary member of the Paris Jockey Club. But what was a Central European doing here now that France was at war? Was it true that the old aristocracies ignored national frontiers as blithely as Communists even in wartime?

They were all sitting around a hearth, watching a dying fire as they drank after-dinner coffee. It was strong and hot and black. Patrick was grateful for his cup. He had had no dinner and the long drive from the old ramparts had tired him.

When he began to tell them about Celia, Clovis cut him short. "Lucien gave me the gist of all this on the telephone. I wish there was something I could do to help, but I'm afraid there's nothing."

"Can't you at least tell me whom I should ask for at the Préfecture or the Sûreté?"

"You'll waste precious time if you go to either one of them. The French police are too preoccupied to function normally tonight, and who can blame them? If they should start an investigation, they may not be able to finish it. The most realistic thing would be to wait until the Germans get here and then approach them."

Patrick was speechless.

"I can see that the idea does not appeal to you." Clovis' tone was wry. "I confess it does not appeal to me either, but what else can you do? I'm leaving Paris myself as soon as I can. I only came back here to save my collection of paintings. I will not let my Monets and Cézannes fall into the hands of General Goering."

"It will be easier for you to talk to the Germans than it would be for us," said Ambrosine. "After all, you are a neutral. They want to keep America out of the war, if they can. They might be quite willing to help you. Why don't you apply to them through your embassy as soon as they get here?"

When Patrick did not answer immediately, she went on. "Are you afraid that your cousin is still with Mr. Radetzkoy? And are you afraid that he may have a police record?"

"Something like that has crossed my mind," said Patrick. "It might not do Celia any good if I drew Nazi attention to her association with Radetzkoy. Don't they believe in guilt by association? And not just in political cases either?"

"What makes you think Radetzkoy may have a police record?" asked Clovis.

Ambrosine answered for Patrick before he could speak. "Isn't it obvious? Monsieur Radetzkoy wins too much at cards for him to be an honest man."

"Have you any idea how he does it?" asked Patrick.

"No, and that's what makes him so utterly fascinating." Ambrosine became animated. A delicate flush in her pale cheeks made her eyes brighter than ever. "I watched both him and your cousin every moment during those last games. I was on the lookout for any signaling by word or gesture. We used fresh packs after every other hand at my suggestion. Whenever he was shuffling or dealing, I never took my eyes away from his hands.

"We all know that cardsharps are conjurors who distract the eye from what they are really doing by some feint. I thought that if I kept that in mind and watched his hands all the time, I could catch him, but I couldn't. He's not a cardsharp. He's a real magician. It's not cheating. It's black magic."

Monsieur Konrad spoke for the first time.

"How that would interest Adolf Hitler!"

Patrick turned to look at him. He was sitting in the shadows apart from the others gathered around the hearth.

"Are you serious?"

"But, yes. Didn't you know? Hitler surrounds himself secretly with clairvoyants and mediums and soothsayers. The only reason some of his laws discourage their open practice is that he does not want ordinary men and women to have access to such power.

"Hitler himself was born in Braumau-am-Inn in a region on the Austro-Hungarian border that has had a tradition of occultism for centuries. It was there that Dr. von Schrenck-Notzing experimented with something he called 'ectoplasm.' He also found two of his most remarkable mediums there, Willi and Rudi Schneider, and another medium who was a cousin of Hitler's."

"Isn't Hitler a sort of medium himself?" said Ambrosine.

"As a boy he was called *mondsüchtig.* Literally it means moonstruck, but it is also a word for sleepwalking, often the first step in a medium's career. Many Germans believe he is a Rasputin who hypnotizes crowds instead of tsarinas. He does cast a Pied Piper spell over a crowd. He

103

draws them into his own trance where they have to share his delusions.

"And that's not all. Half Germany believes he escaped the bomb in the Bürgerbräukeller at Munich last November because his daemon told him to rush out of the building eight minutes before the bomb went off, long · before he was scheduled to leave."

"It's a pity he didn't use his clairvoyance to save the lives of those followers of his who were killed when the bomb went off," said Clovis.

Konrad smiled. "In an emergency Herr Hitler is apt to think of number one."

"This is fantastic," Ambrosine said to Konrad. "Are you suggesting that Radetzkoy may use some kind of second sight when he plays cards?"

"Why not?" returned Konrad. "Weren't cards used for divination long before anyone ever thought of playing games with them or betting on them? Cards began as fortune-telling arrows. These, enlarged and decorated, became the first cards and then, some say, the first books."

"In Korea, wasn't it?" said Clovis. "When I was in Vietnam a friend showed me archaic, Korean playing cards. I was surprised to see how much they looked like our own western face cards."

Patrick wondered how these people could sit and talk about prehistoric cards and Hitler's talents as a shaman when every second that ticked away made it less likely that he would find Celia before the Nazis arrived.

Of course she was his cousin, not theirs, and more than a cousin to him now.

He looked from one face to another. They were all closed. He was not going to get help here.

When he got down to the street, he was a little surprised to see Dr. Bertrand's car still at the curb, and Jules, as resilient as ever, hopping out to open the door.

Patrick had forgotten Jules as well as the car. Now he looked at the man's sharp, intelligent face with sudden interest.

"No luck?" said Jules.

"No luck." How did Jules know that Patrick needed luck? "Did Dr. Bertrand tell you why I was coming here this evening?"

"He dropped a few hints. From the way you look now I gather these people are not going to help you find Miss McNeill."

"They can't help me, or so they say."

Jules eased the car to a stop against the curb. His eyes were watching Patrick in the rearview mirror.

"Then it's up to you and me, m'sieu."

"You and me?"

"There's no one else, is there?" returned Jules. "Luckily I have the evening off. Shall I drive up Saint Germain to the Deux Magots where we can sit down with a little glass and make a plan?"

Patrick remembered that Jules was the man who had disposed of two thugs in Normandy with remarkable efficiency.

"If you have a plan, let's hear it. Drive on."

12
Café des Deux Magots

Patrick passed the Café des Deux Magots whenever he walked from his home in the Place du Panthéon to his office in the Place Vendôme. He had rarely seen more than half a dozen people at the tables on the terrace outside. As he had not been born on the Austro-Bavarian border where everybody sees the future, he had no intimation that after the war someone named Sartre would make the café fashionable.

It was too cool and too dark for most people to sit outside tonight so they had the terrace largely to themselves. They could not see the two Chinese grotesques that gave the place its name, but they had a close view of the oldest church in Paris, Saint Germain des Près.

Patrick ordered fines for Jules and himself and then said, "Now tell me everything that happened in Normandy."

"From the very beginning?"

"Please."

Jules' story did not diverge from Celia's until he came to the point where he was left alone in the road with Pépé and Gogo.

"I herded my two sorry prisoners into their own car until the police arrived and took over. Then I made my statement and told the flics they could find other witnesses at Dr. Bertrand's villa in the morning."

"What next?"

"The sergeant on duty was a good fellow. He got one of the other flics to run me home in a police car. I went in the service entrance at the back without disturbing anybody. I was quite surprised to see Monsieur le Marquis, somewhat the worse for wear, mooning around in the kitchen, the last place I ever expected to see him. He asked me if I'd seen Henri and I said 'No' and was there anything I could do for him? He said 'No, thank you.' Unlike Bertrand, Monsieur le Marquis is always polite. Then he wandered off someplace by himself, and I went upstairs to bed. I did not see Monsieur Kyros then. I have no idea when he was murdered. I knew nothing about the Affair Kyros until the next morning when Monsieur le Docteur found his body in the road and called the police.

"Do you realize that if I had gone to the front door I would have discovered Kyros' body then? But there's a separate lane that leads off the highway to the back door, so I didn't have to go anywhere near Kyros' body to get into the house."

"When was the body discovered?"

"Not until noon when Monsieur le Marquis and Madame his wife left for Paris. By that time it was difficult to establish the actual time of death because the body had been left outdoors in the cold for so long. At that time all the police could establish was that Monsieur

Kyros had left the house alone, on foot, just before dawn, apparently looking for his lost ring."

"And no one thought of going as far as the hollow to look for him?"

"They weren't that worried. After all he was a grown man and the neighborhood has always been quiet."

"Did the police have any leads? Or don't you know?"

"I know they found a place in the woods where they thought the sniper must have been standing when he fired. That's why they think he must have been a good marksman. It was quite a distance from Kyros' body."

"And the police didn't hold you?"

"There was no reason to hold anybody and Monsieur le Docteur wanted to take off for Paris as soon as possible. You can imagine what a brouhaha that was. Flics all over the place, still no sign of Henri, and me left to do all the packing and closing of the house by myself; but what would you? Somebody had to do it."

"When did you leave?"

"Two days later. I loaded the car in the morning and by two we were on the road to Paris."

The waiter brought the little glasses of brandy. Patrick looked up at a scatter of stars above the old church and asked himself, silently, what the hell am I doing here, sitting on the terrace of a Parisian café late at night, talking to the chauffeur of a man I scarcely know about a cousin I scarcely know while a German army is within a few days of Paris?

"Who do you think killed Kyros?"

"I have no idea, m'sieu."

"Why do you think he was killed?"

"How can I say?"

"Would you be surprised if I told you that Radetzkoy

found the body before anyone else? And that someone shot at him, too?"

"And killed him?"

"No, but he was wounded."

"Where?"

"In the knee."

"Ugh." Jules shuddered. "That's not as dangerous as a stomach wound, but it hurts more. This marksman must be good. It's hard to hit a target as small as a knee at a distance."

"You think the sniper shot Radetzkoy in the knee cap purposely?"

"It's a place you'd try to hit if you wanted to immobilize a man without killing him. This joker must be a good marksman or he wouldn't have been able to kill Kyros. You know he's pretty smart, doing his fancy shooting just now, when the Germans are nearly here."

"You mean he's hiding a murder in a battle like hiding a leaf in a forest?"

"Isn't he? There's been bombing and machine-gunning and sniping all over the place. Who's going to look for a single murderer in a mess like this? Who can say that Kyros was shot at such and such a time or such and such a place, when everybody is shooting at everybody else. everywhere, all the time? How can the police care now about the death of one man? We're all more interested now in finding out how many people escaped death than in finding out who killed Aristides Kyros. Poor devil, he chose the wrong time and place to be murdered. Any more questions?"

"Dozens. Did the sniper kill Kyros because he mistook Kyros for Radetzkoy at that distance? Did he try to repair his mistake by shooting at Radetzkoy later? Or did the sniper kill Kyros deliberately and only shoot at Radetz-

109

koy and Celia later to keep them from discovering the murder while he, the murderer, was still in the neighborhood? Any answers?"

"No. I'd just be guessing. Guesses don't work in this game."

Patrick tried another tack.

"No word from Henri since he left?"

"None."

"Any idea why he decamped?"

"I have a suspicion." Jules lips curled in a slow, subtle, very French smile.

"Why?"

"Henri was out of a job. Monsieur le Docteur was closing the villa for the duration and going back to Paris. He had told Henri to find another job and had given him three months wages. Pretty short notice after fourteen years' service. Henri hadn't much chance of finding another job. Everyone's cutting down on staff because of the war."

"He might have found a war job."

"At his age? All that cash Radetzkoy won at the casino must have been quite a temptation for Henri."

"Had he a car?"

"Not one of his own, but he was allowed to use one of Bertrand's cars for errands in the village. That car is missing now."

"Where did Henri come from?"

"Paris."

"Have the police any theories about who killed Kyros?"

"If they have, they didn't tell me. They just asked me questions."

"Sometimes a question is a giveaway," said Patrick. "It can tell you what is going on in the questioner's

110

mind. Were there any questions like that?"

"No, just routine stuff. Why had Henri scrammed? Where would he be likely to go and—"

"Jules."

"M'sieu?"

"Did you tell the police where he would be likely to go?"

"Me? Of course not. I don't like Henri much, but I'd never squeal on him to the flics."

"Will you squeal on him to me?"

Jules' eyes narrowed. "You think Henri knows where mademoiselle is?"

"It's one possibility. I'd better tell you I talked to her yesterday at my office in the Place Vendôme."

"You did! Then—"

"Hold it. I lost her afterward. She and Radetzkoy were going to meet me for dinner. They never appeared. They were not at the hotel where she had said they were staying. But I simply do not believe she would have broken a date with me without telephoning. Not if she were a free agent."

"And you think Henri is mixed up in it?"

"I'm beginning to."

"I can figure Henri taking cash, but why would he handicap himself with a wounded man and a girl?"

"I have no idea, but he's the only lead I have, so I've got to look for him. Have you any idea where he might be now?"

"There's one possibility, but it's not very likely."

Patrick made an effort to keep impatience out of his voice. "And what is that?"

"Henri did tell me once that he had an aunt. . . . Or was it a great aunt?"

"Never mind that now. What about her?"

111

"He said she had a job as a concierge."

"Where?"

"In Paris, in the Latin Quarter. One of those buildings that let furnished rooms to students. She lives in the basement, I think."

"Could she keep guests in basement rooms?"

"Not in the kind of basement rooms they give to concierges, but Henri might get rooms for himself in her building at short notice."

"He couldn't get a lease at a day or so's notice."

"Furnished rooms aren't let on leases. They're not apartments. They have no bathrooms or kitchens. You can take them by the month or even by the week."

"Or the day?"

"No, they're respectable. They're meant for students. Young people move around a lot, so there are usually some vacancies."

"Then if you'll give me this aunt's address, I can—"

"I can't remember it. It's something to do with history."

"What Paris street name hasn't?"

"But this is really old history. Something unpleasant about it, too. When I reach for it, I almost catch it, and then it's gone."

Patrick believed that only conscious neglect will bring the unconscious to heel, so he tried to distract Jules.

"There's one other lead I have, a very small one. Something Kyros said to Celia just before he died: *der rauchende Spiegel.*"

Jules looked so blank, Patrick hastened to translate: "The smoking mirror."

"Why should a British subject born in Crete speak German when he's dying?"

112

"Perhaps he was talking about something most people think of as German."

Jules snapped his fingers. "Got it!"

"The meaning of the smoking mirror?"

"No, the address. It's a little spot in the Latin Quarter called the Place de l'Estrapade."

"What?"

Jules was watching Patrick's face. "So you've heard of it?"

"Of course I have. I live just around the corner in the Place du Panthéon."

"Coincidence?"

"They do happen. Obviously Henri went there because of his aunt. He knew nothing about me. Even Celia didn't know where I was."

"What happens now?" asked Jules.

Patrick looked at his watch. "We go to the Place de l'Estrapade and get Celia out, if she's still there."

"We? Monsieur is coming with me?"

"Had you thought of going alone?"

"Of course." Jules was amused. "You're the first boss I've ever worked with who wanted to go with me on one of these crazy little errands. You're quite sure you want to?"

"Quite sure."

Patrick signaled the waiter, wondering just what sort of errands Jules performed for Bertrand.

"Most bosses seem to feel I'm expendable and they're not," explained Jules. "Some day I may write my memoirs."

It was Patrick's turn to be amused. "Perhaps a mere threat to do so might be more profitable than any book."

When they left, Jules did not drive up the Rue Soufflot

113

as Patrick would have done. He threaded the maze of little streets near it until he came out in the Rue des Fossés Saint Jacques. This led him to the Place de l'Estrapade without his having to pass the policeman on sentry duty in front of the Mairie of the Fifth Arrondissement.

"You know your city," said Patrick.

"I'm Paris born and bred." Jules spoke with the pride that often makes poverty in Paris more attractive to a Parisian than wealth in the provinces.

"I was born in one of the working-class slums," he went on. "The first war shook me loose. Nothing else could have done so. I was just old enough to be called up in the last year, 1918. I stayed in the army after the war and rose to be a commissioned officer for a while, assigned to intelligence.

"At last I got fed up and got out only to find I could not go back to factory life. Those were bad years. I might have drifted into one of the rackets. The job with Monsieur le Docteur came along just in time in the thirties."

"How did you meet him?

"At his clinic. I was having a sort of breakdown."

"So Dr. Bertrand takes charity patients?"

"They all take charity patients when they're young, and he was young then as well as I. That's how doctors get their guinea pigs. Even the great Dr. Charcot, Freud's teacher, made his reputation through clinical experiments with whores at the Salpêtrière. They don't call it experiment, of course. They call it treatment. But the things they try on charity patients wouldn't be tried on paying patients.

"Dr. Bertrand is more sensible than most of them. He saw at once there was nothing wrong with me that couldn't be cured by a steady job and regular meals.

Luckily he needed someone like me, an ex-intelligence officer whom he could turn into a bodyguard and errand boy. In our society there is one person who never lacks employment—the man with a gun."

Jules had stopped the car. Now he opened the glove compartment and took out a revolver which he slipped into his jacket pocket.

"Have you papers for that?"

"Oh, yes. Dr. Bertrand is very punctilious about that sort of thing. I wish you'd stay in the car now."

"Why?"

"There's no knowing what we may find inside, and there won't be time for us to consult each other once we get in."

"I'll follow your lead," said Patrick promptly. "After all you're more used to this sort of thing than I am. I have only one proviso."

"What's that?"

"Don't kill anybody."

"If monsieur thinks for one moment that I am capable of—"

"Jules, I think you are capable of anything."

13
Place de l'Estrapade

They left the car in the Rue des Fossés Saint Jacques and groped their way across the little Place de l'Estrapade. In the starlight, Patrick could barely see the four stunted, city trees he had noticed by day, their leaves motionless in the still air. There was nothing anywhere to suggest the tortures that had once been enacted here. Only historians remembered them now.

Jules led the way to the third house in the row facing them. Its windows were all dark at this hour. He fumbled with the door and found a bell beside it. He put a finger on the button and held it there.

It seemed a full minute or even a little longer before a light bloomed behind dark curtains in a window and a clicking noise came from the door. Jules pushed it open.

They were in a narrow lobby. One dim electric bulb, no more than twenty-five watts, diluted the darkness, turning it into a muddy twilight.

At the far end a bunk, like those on small boats, was

116

separated from the hall by a panel of opaque glass. This panel had been pushed to one side. An old woman's face filled the opening. Patrick was aware of scant, tangled, iron-gray hair and eyes drunk with sleep. A voice, clogged with mucus, quavered, "Henri?"

Jules spoke in a soothing whisper.

"It's all right. Go back to sleep."

But this only roused her. She spoke more sharply now.

"You're not Henri and you're not alone."

"No, but we are friends of someone who lives here, Henri Duvernois."

"No one of that name here."

A liver-spotted hand with swollen knuckles was holding the edge of the glass panel. It clenched now.

Jules paused deliberately, a man trying to decide which of several possible cards to play, then he went on.

"I have a message for Henri from his employer."

"A likely story."

"He is also my employer, Monsieur le Docteur Bertrand."

"Oh . . ." The hand relaxed. "Why didn't you say so in the first place? Monsieur Duvernois is on the sixth floor, door facing the head of the stair."

"Thank you, madame."

But she didn't answer. She had already fallen back in her bunk, pulling the glass panel shut as she did so.

Jules led the way past the bunk, past some mailboxes, through a door to a steep, spiral staircase, disappearing into the dimness above their heads. More twenty-five-watt bulbs diluted the dark on each landing.

"We'll have to hurry now," said Jules. "Lights in these places are turned on whenever the front door is opened at night, but they're wired to an automatic timer, and

117

whoever sets it never allows enough time to reach the top floor. This saves the landlord all of two and a half sous."

"Didn't you bring a flashlight?"

"I forgot. It's a long time since I've been in a place like this."

The risers were so high and the spiral so tight that climbing these stairs was almost like climbing a mountain.

"If Henri had any sense, he would have told that old hag not to admit anyone who asked for him or tell anyone he was here," said Jules.

"Who is she?"

"Probably a maid-of-all-work employed by Henri's aunt, the concierge."

A sudden, sharp crack interrupted them.

"What was that?" cried Patrick.

"Backfire in the street probably."

Patrick went back to what he was saying. "Do you mean she works all day and then spends all night in a bunk the size of a dog kennel where her sleep is interrupted every time anyone wants to come in?"

"Didn't you know about that?" asked Jules. "It's plain to be seen you have no friends among the really poor students in Paris, the ones from Central Europe and Japan. This is how they live."

The sound of running feet came down the stair from above, rattling like castanets.

"Somebody's in a hurry," said Jules. "Better stand back."

They flattened themselves as best they could against the curved wall.

The footsteps sounded closer now, as if they were just beyond the next curve in the wall above.

Patrick was looking up to see what kind of man or

118

woman would descend this tight spiral at such breakneck speed, when the lights went out and he was plunged into blinding darkness.

Before he could speak, an invisible body collided with him knocking the breath out of his lungs.

"Mer-de . . ." It was a hoarse whisper, jarred out of someone's throat by shock.

There was no slackening of speed. The frantic feet crashed on, growing fainter as they receded, leaving a sweetish smell behind.

"Quick!"

Patrick heard Jules starting in pursuit as fast as he could in the darkness. Patrick tried to follow. As they rounded the bottom curve in the stair, the lights came on again and the front door slammed.

Jules ran to it and tore it open. Patrick looked over his shoulder, but by that time the Place de l'Estrapade was empty in the starlight.

Jules closed the door and turned towards the bunk, brows bent together, eyes sharper than ever.

"Who was that who just left?"

The old woman quavered. "I didn't see anybody."

"The lights came on when he opened the front door. You must have seen him then. He had just passed us on the stair."

"I was asleep."

"He was making a lot of noise. He must have wakened you."

"I didn't hear a thing. I was too tired."

Patrick touched Jules' arm and tilted his head towards the stair.

"Better not waste any more time here."

"I suppose you're right."

On the stair Jules whispered to Patrick. "I almost sym-

119

pathize with flics who get rough with witnesses who won't talk."

"You think she saw him?"

"I know she did, but no one will ever get it out of her if she's afraid to talk. Did you notice anything distinctive about him in the dark? Anything you would recognize if you met him again?"

"That *mer-de* sounded like the Midi."

"There are a lot of people in the Midi. You can't identify one man that way."

"There was something else. I can't put a finger on it now. Just a feeling in the air."

They were nearly at the sixth floor when the lights went out again.

They felt their way along a wall until they came to the door facing the stairs. There was a faint light on the landing. It came from a door, standing ajar, facing the head of the stair. Jules took out his revolver. "Stay behind me. There may be a reception committee here."

The room within was dingy and dimly lighted with blackout curtains drawn across two tall windows. A man was lying on the floor in an awkward position. A worn rug was crumpled in folds under his feet as if he had slipped on it before he went down. His eyes, open and empty, told them he was dead before they saw the bullet hole in his forehead.

"You know him?" asked Patrick.

"Yes. It's Henri."

There was another door opposite, and someone was pounding on it from the other side.

Patrick had to kick the lock three times before it gave.

Gun in hand, Jules pushed the door open and jumped

120

to one side, avoiding a possible line of fire, but there were no shots.

"Celia . . . ?"

Patrick took a step forward and stopped.

She was standing beyond the open door. A stranger was holding her head against his shoulder so she could not see the dead man on the floor. Patrick did not have to be told that this was Sergei Radetzkoy.

His thoughts jeered at him. Why are you surprised? Of course they're lovers. They've shared danger for over a month now on the most intimate terms, in a world where everything is changing.

There was no comfort in such thoughts at all.

14

Mont Sainte Geneviève

It was still dark when Patrick opened his eyes sleepily. For a moment he was bemused to find himself on a couch in the little room he used as home office. Then memory came flooding back, and he was so wide awake that he knew he could not go back to sleep again that night.

He looked at the watch he had left on the desk. He was not surprised to see it was four in the morning. Every time he went to sleep with something on his mind, he would sleep soundly for a few hours and then wake absurdly early as if conscience was rationing the amount of sleep it would allow him until his problem was solved.

He had no desire for breakfast or even coffee, but he did crave a cigarette. For some years now he had held himself down to six a day, two after each meal, and it usually worked, but not this morning.

There were no cigarettes in this room. He would have to go into the living room where Jules was sleeping to get any.

Moving as quietly as he could, he found cigarettes on the living-room chimneypiece and lit one.

Jules, on the sofa, did not stir. Sleep had smoothed the lines from his face. Lips parted, eyes lidded, he looked younger now and almost innocent, but no man could be called innocent who had got them out of their tight corner last night as smoothly as he had done.

It was he who had pointed out that only one witness, the old woman, had talked to them or seen them enter the building. Both times she was half asleep. She was too old to have sharp sight or hearing. Like all the really poor she would be automatically hostile to the law. Even if she did recognize them later, she would never identify them to the police.

When they got downstairs, she was still asleep or feigning sleep. Perhaps the shot fired six floors above had not wakened her. Perhaps she did not wish to know what was going on.

With a quick gesture, Jules motioned them outside. "See? There'll be no witness to connect us with the crime here."

"But she must have seen whoever it was collided with me on the stair in the dark when he got to the lobby," said Patrick. "Shouldn't we ask her about him again?"

"About the murderer? Wild horses wouldn't drag anything about him out of her now. The only sensible thing for us to do is to get out before someone else discovers the body and calls the police. Isn't your apartment just around the corner? We can hole up there for the rest of the night."

"I suppose you realize we're breaking the law if we don't report this to the police ourselves?" said Patrick.

"Forget you're a member of the bar for just one night," retorted Jules. "That is if you want to get your

123

young cousin out of here before the Nazis arrive."

So they had come to Patrick's apartment. He had put Celia in his own room and Radetzkoy in the guest room. It did seem a little absurd when he remembered that Sergei and Celia had been sharing the cellar of a bombed-out farmhouse for several weeks and were obviously in love. So why was he separating them now?

If anyone had asked him that question, he would have answered that life in France had taught him manners and appearances are more socially useful than laws or morals because they are behavioristic. They are concerned with what we do, not just what we believe or feel. This makes them the only practical form of compassion and the one discipline that stands fast when laws and morals break down.

He understood now why the old régime in France expected its husbands to overlook adultery as long as appearances were kept up, but insisted that any man who dared to lay a finger on the back of a wife's chair in public should be challenged to a duel immediately. Perhaps the Chinese were right. Perhaps saving face is the one thing that makes human society possible at all.

Even while Patrick was thinking these things he realized that they were strange thoughts for a lawyer and a Bostonian. Was this war going to bring as many social changes as the last one?

"I'd like one of those cigarettes."

Jules was sitting up on the couch, dark hair tousled and spiky, eyes sharp as ever.

Patrick gave him a Gitane Vizir.

"No Gauloises?"

"I avoid poison gas. How about coffee?"

"Not yet." Jules inhaled luxuriously even though the cigarette was too mild for his taste. "What time is it?"

124

"A little after four. Sorry if I woke you."

"I'm glad you did. You and I have a few things to talk over."

Jules pushed a pillow between his back and the wall and leaned against it, both hands clasped behind his head. The cigarette at one corner of his mouth was cocked at a rakish angle.

"Do you realize that we are now involved in two murders and an attempted murder?"

"Something like that has crossed my mind."

"It all boils down to four things: Who killed Kyros and why? Who killed Henri and why? Who tried to kill your cousin and Radetzkoy when they found Kyros' body? And last, but not least, what is the connection between Radetzkoy and Kyros?"

"When we were all talking after we got back here last night, I tried to see some sort of pattern, but I couldn't. It's like a picture puzzle with several pieces missing. I wonder if there's any way you and I can fill in some of the gaps."

"You might try asking Sergei some of those questions. He's been in this from the beginning. I haven't."

"I doubt if Monsieur Radetzkoy will answer any questions satisfactorily," said Jules. "He's hiding something, and when you're doing that, you don't talk about anything."

"There is a fifth question," said Patrick. "Why did Henri hold Sergei and Celia as prisoners?"

"Money."

"That's what Celia thinks. She said last night that if Sergei had taken a check for his winnings at the Casino in Trouville, this would never have happened. He asked for cash because he thought the banks might close for a day or so during the hiatus between invasion and occupation. He used some of that cash for stakes in the game at the villa. Henri saw then how much cash Sergei had with him. The temptation was too much for a man who had just lost his job and had little hope of getting another one soon. He'd been listening to his radio in the kitchen. He knew how badly things were going."

"Then we agree Henri is just a grace note?"

"I'd say he caused a crossruff between his little crime and a bigger one and got himself killed because he got in somebody's way."

"How did he manage to overpower Radetzkoy and Celia? It was two against one in their favor."

Patrick leapt to Celia's defense. "But Henri was the one who had the gun. He could always control one of them by threatening to kill the other."

"How did he catch up with them on the road?"

"He tracked them by asking people along the way if they had seen a young girl and a man with a limp traveling together in a green Peugeot. Everyone tried to help him because everyone thought he was a refugee who had been separated from his family. He finally ran them down in the farmhouse cellar. At first he posed as a friend, hiding them from the Germans, finding food for them, keeping them under shelter when there was bombing."

"The faithful old retainer bit?"

"I'm afraid so."

Jules grinned. "We all fall for it because it's so flattering. Even Dr. Bertrand couldn't believe Henri had deserted him. He kept saying, 'But the man's absolutely devoted to me. He's been with me for years.' I suppose he thinks I'm absolutely devoted to him and look at me now, sitting here jawing with you when I should be reporting for duty."

126

"Not at four A.M., I hope. Why are you asking me all these questions about Henri?"

"I'm trying to find out who else could have had a motive for killing him besides Radetzkoy and Miss McNeill. We know they didn't do it because they were locked in that back room when the shot was fired. We had to break the lock to get them out. Remember?"

"I'll never forget it."

"What else did your cousin tell you last night? Anything important?"

"Not really."

"Tell me."

"She said Henri was quite clever about getting them to go to Paris with him. He told them they'd be better off in Paris because it would be declared an open city.

"He said that as soon as the roads were safe he would take them both in his car to the Place de l'Estrapade where they were sure to get rooms cheaply because his aunt was in charge of the building there. They had no idea then that the car he called 'his' was stolen from Dr. Bertrand.

"Once inside the apartment at the Place de l'Estrapade, he threatened them with his gun, imprisoned them in a locked room, and took the cash Sergei had won at the casino in Trouville. Of course he was furious when he discovered that all Sergei's winnings at the villa had been paid in checks made out to Sergei. For by then Sergei's infected knee was so bad that he had a high fever and his mind was wandering. In that condition, he could not be made to understand that he must endorse the checks, so Henri forged Sergei's signature.

"Celia had told him about me. His idea was that she could get the checks cashed at Morgan's on the strength

127

of the forged signature if she could get me to vouch for her there.

"Henri didn't dare come with her to see me because that would mean leaving Sergei alone, and there was always a possibility that he might come to his senses and escape or go to the police.

"Henri tried to safeguard himself by intimidating Celia. He told her that if she told me the truth, he would kill me. She didn't know whether he was capable of murder or not, but he had already shown himself so callous that she didn't dare take a chance on what he might or might not do."

"Why didn't she just throw herself on your mercy and ask you for help?"

"Because Henri had anticipated that. He told her that if the police appeared in the Place de l'Estrapade while she was gone, he would kill Sergei immediately. He also gave her a time limit for getting back. If she were not there on the dot, Sergei would die. I noticed her watching the clock while she was in my office. Of course I had no idea what a strain she was under at that time."

"Then why didn't she get you to vouch for her and cash the damn checks?"

"She said that when it came to the point she just couldn't make herself drag me into such a dangerous situation while she couldn't risk telling me what was going on."

"Henri can't have been too pleased when she came back with the checks uncashed."

"He wasn't. It was then he locked her in the inner room with Sergei. All the rest of the afternoon she could hear Henri pacing the floor in the outer room. She thinks he was trying to work out some other way of getting those checks cashed without any risk to himself. . . . How about some coffee now?"

They went into the kitchen to make the coffee, but the change of scene did not bring about a change of subject. Jules was still worrying the puzzle like a terrier with a rat.

"Do you know what a catalyst is?"

"A chemical that sets off the reactions of other chemicals to each other."

"Do you realize who has been the catalyst in all these killings and crimes and attempted crimes? The enigmatic Monsieur Radetzkoy."

"Enigmatic?"

"Prepare for a small shock," said Jules. "Or has it occurred to you already that Radetzkoy may have something to do with British Intelligence?

"That whole scene on the pier at Dieppe and later, at the pension, has the flavor of a charade. Were enemy agents watching? Was Inspector Grosjean told to look out for Sergei and detain him in order to draw attention to him? Nothing was what it seemed. Even Sergei himself was acting the part of a seedy adventurer. Your little cousin was the innocent bystander, wandering between the lines on a battlefield."

"And what was Sergei?"

"The tethered goat staked out to bring the tiger into the open. He was probably told to land without a passport so everybody could see just how stateless and vulnerable he was."

"And who is the tiger?"

"I don't know, but I believe we should be looking for somebody who thinks like a Nazi. This smells like a Nazi crime."

"Does Kyros fit into this new pattern?"

"His job was selling works of art. That involves travel

129

and a knowledge of foreign languages. Suggest anything to you?"

"Perfect cover for an intelligence agent."

"He was probably working with Radetzkoy."

"But he went out of his way to discredit Sergei when he talked to Celia at the pension."

"Would you expect him to advertise the fact that he and Radetzkoy were allies? I think Kyros was Radetzkoy's line of communication with England, and he was killed to isolate Radetzkoy, the way you cut a telephone wire to isolate a house."

Before Patrick had time to digest all this, Jules went on briskly: "What do you know about Hitler?"

"Mostly what I hear on radio and read in newspapers."

Jules began to speak in a slow, mesmeric rhythm:

> "On bitter nights I often go
> To Wotan's oak in the quiet glade
> To weave a union with dark forces . . ."

"Did Hitler write that?" asked Patrick.

"In 1917, when he was in the trenches. It tells us everything."

There was a long silence as Patrick thought about the revelations of the last few hours.

He had started the night with a tough little chauffeur, a city sparrow who referred to policemen as flics. He was ending it with another man one who quoted Hitler's verse and talked fluently on a variety of uncommon topics.

If Sergei was enigmatic, what was Jules himself?

Patrick reached for another cigarette. He had stopped counting them some time ago.

130

"Did you know some anthropologists have stopped calling primitive societies primitive?" said Jules. "The word 'primitive' had become so abusive, they decided to say 'archaic' instead, but actually the archaic or primitive is an essential stage of development which all cultures, whether they are civilized now or not, must pass through at one time or another.

"It is healthy for a young society to be primitive just as it's healthy for a child to be childlike. The trouble starts when an old society tries to revert to the primitive-archaic. That's as disastrous as second childhood in a grown man, and I think that is what is happening to Germany under Hitler.

"The swastika is as old as sun worship, and, by Hitler's own personal order, the Nazis display the swastika that spins counterclockwise, the old symbol of black magic. Blood and soil is a primordial cult. What is *ein Reich, ein Volk, ein Führer* but an archaic war chant? In their social childhood all cultures define good and evil in terms of their own clan. 'I kill my enemy, good. My enemy kills me, evil.' That is Nazi morality, too. Now think a minute and tell me: What is a universal factor in all early societies, whether they be European or Asiatic or African?"

When Patrick hesitated, Jules answered his own question.

"Magic. And what is the oldest kind of leader? A magus or shaman. And what is the most important gift of a true magus?"

"You tell me," said Patrick.

"His ability to foresee the future. Many Germans believe that is the secret of Hitler's rise to power and all his victories."

"Jules, I can't believe this is happening in modern, scientific Germany."

131

Jules laughed. "You'd be surprised how many hard-headed businessmen in modern, scientific Paris always consult some astrologer before making an important move on the Bourse. The point is not what you or I or Anatole France believes, but what Hitler and his Nazis believe. If you wanted to plant an undercover agent close to Hitler, how would you set about it?"

"I suppose I'd try to take advantage of some blind spot in Hitler himself."

"And what is Hitler's blind spot?"

Patrick thought a moment.

"Wotan's oak?"

"Exactly."

"Sergei?"

"Who else? Hitler would hardly accept a Frenchman or an Englishman in this role at this stage of the game, but some White Russians are pro-Nazi. They see Nazism as anticommunism and dream of a counterrevolution in Russia backed by Germany. And don't forget that Russia has its own occultist tradition, ranging from scientists and philosophers like Aksakoff and Ouspensky to less rational prophets like the two fascinating Siberians, Gurdjieff and Rasputin."

"It would be a pretty grim risk for Sergei."

"He'd have to have the nerve of the devil, but it could be done."

"Cards?"

"What better way to advertise clairvoyance than by word of mouth, always so quick and effective? When an occultist hears about inexplicable luck at cards, he always thinks of precognition. He knows cards were tools of divination before money and betting were invented. He remembers that Rhine turned to cards when he made the first statistical tests of ESP."

132

"To get away with it Sergei would have to have either a foolproof method of cheating or an undetectable mathematical system."

"But think what dazzling opportunities he'd have to feed them misinformation. If he were there now, they'd be asking him to look into the future and tell them whether he saw an invasion of England or an invasion of Russia."

This startled Patrick. "What about the Hitler-Stalin pact?"

"Did you think that was going to last? They're already discussing the invasion date, probably July, 1941."

"Doesn't Hitler know you can read the future in the past? Napoleon tried to fight England and Russia at the same time. It didn't work."

"But Hitler's magi have told him it will work this time. They say the universe is based on a conflict of ice and fire. This doctrine of eternal ice is known in Germany as *Welteislehre*. Men like Horbiger, Haushofer, and Rosenberg have convinced Hitler that German magi are now in command of the ice, so the cold of a Russian winter cannot stop the fire of a German invasion. Russia is ice. Germany is fire. Therefore, Germany will win."

"Are you quite sure that British intelligence has not already planted somebody among Hitler's magi?"

Jules laughed.

A voice spoke from the doorway.

"Don't laugh. This isn't funny."

Celia stood on the threshold, barefoot, hair damp from a shower, enveloped in a dressing gown of Patrick's much too big for her. She looked as lost as those heroines in movies of the thirties who are so often forced to spend a night in the hero's bedroom by crisis or circumstance, but never inclination.

133

She dropped into a chair and looked up at Patrick.

"Do you think I haven't wondered about Sergei ever since I first met him? I've known he must be involved in something horrible ever since Kyros was killed. Whatever it is, it can't be his fault, so I've never asked him about it.

"I heard what you were saying just now. Do you really believe that he's a spy? And that there's a plan to introduce him to occultists around Hitler so he can exploit Hitler's credulity?"

"It's one possibility," said Patrick.

"Have you thought what such a plan would do to Sergei himself? If he pretends he can predict the future, he'll make some slip sooner or later. They'll investigate him then and find out he's a fake and hang him as a spy."

"He could always pretend that he had suddenly lost a power of prediction he once had," said Jules.

"If he did they'd work on him to bring it back with drugs and hypnosis and brutality. He'd just die slowly instead of quickly."

Jules looked at Patrick obliquely. "She could be right."

Patrick surrendered.

"What do you want me to do, Celia?"

"Get Sergei out of here before the Nazis arrive. That's more important than getting me out. They've nothing against me, but they may have something against him already. Why else was Kyros shot?"

Jules intervened again. "If he tries to leave after they get here, they may just arrest him and ship him to Germany."

"Then he must leave now, today," cried Celia.

"Don't panic," said Jules. "They won't be here for another day or so."

Patrick brought coffee from the kitchen.

134

Celia took her cup over to a window.

"It must be nearly dawn now," she said. "Let's see what the weather's like."

Jules turned out the lights. Patrick pushed the blackout curtains aside.

Pale, predawn light welled in the room like water. The two men stood beside Celia at the window.

It was neither dark nor light outside. Everything was gray—sky, cobblestones, library, law school, Panthéon.

Celia spoke quietly. "Isn't this the hill where Sainte Geneviève prayed for Attila to spare Paris?"

"The very hill," said Jules. "And Paris was spared, but that was in 451 A.D."

"Since I've lived here, I've had dreams about medieval Paris," said Patrick. "I know they're just a rehash of all the stuff I've been reading, but that doesn't make them any less eerie.

"It's always a winter night. There's a graveyard where the Panthéon is now and woods beyond. You can hear wolves howling in the woods and mothers telling their children never to go as far as the graveyard after dark."

The sky above the dome of the Panthéon was turning a delicate rose.

Suddenly Celia caught Patrick's wrist. "Look . . ."

At first he thought she meant the sky. Then he saw movement below.

A solitary motorcyclist was coming into the empty Place rather slowly from the Rue Cujas.

He crossed the Place at a steady, even pace, making only a little noise.

He wore a gray uniform and heavy boots. His helmet was an unfamiliar shape, curving down low over the nape of his neck. From that height they could not see his face.

135

He turned deliberately and went down the Rue Soufflot towards the Luxembourg Gardens.

"What is he?" asked Celia.

"He looks rather like the point man of a panzer division," answered Patrick.

Jules nodded as if he could not trust himself to speak.

15
Rue des Saules

If Celia had not been advised to stay indoors all day, she might have been quite content to rest. As it was, she became prey to the special anxieties of inactivity as soon as Patrick and Jules went out.

No sound came from the room where Sergei was still sleeping. She might as well have been alone in the place.

She tried to make little activities for herself indoors, but there was not enough to keep her occupied once she had washed breakfast dishes and done a little dusting and sweeping.

She found a few books on Patrick's shelves that were old friends, but even these could not lull a sense of unease heightened by ignorance of what was going on elsewhere. Patrick had urged her to stay away from windows at the front of the house, but the temptation to look out grew stronger every minute. When she finally did, she stood to one side of the window frame where she could hardly be seen from below. She was not the only one staying indoors today. The Place was empty most of the time.

As the uneventful morning wore on, she remembered hearing that thousands of Parisians lived through the French Revolution without ever seeing anyone guillotined or hanged from a lamp post. For the first time she realized that great historical events have little direct impact on the lives of ordinary people. If you had a job to do, or children to care for, and lived away from the center of a city, riot and revolution, invasion and war might pass over your head, hardly noticed except for food shortages and the ever-present background of fear.

When noon came and there was still no sound from Sergei, she slipped into the room where he was sleeping.

He opened his eyes. "Perfect timing. I just woke up."

She leaned down to kiss him and brush the hair from his forehead. "I'll make fresh coffee," she said.

When she came back from the kitchen, he was in the living room, wearing a robe and pajamas Patrick had left out for him. In the pitiless north light, his face was wasted, his cheeks hollow, his eyes sunk in their sockets. Yet when he smiled, she forgot all that and saw only his resilient spirit.

She forced herself to say: "You look better."

"Were you worried about me?"

"I always worry about you because you don't worry about yourself. Somebody has to do it."

He laughed. "I'm tougher than you think. I shan't die young. Did I ever tell you I once dreamed about my own death? It was in an old Roman ruin. So all I have to do is keep out of Italy, and I'll live forever."

He held out his cup for more coffee. "It's awfully quiet here this morning. Where is everybody?"

"Jules went out to see what can be done about getting you and me to England."

"Without passports?"

"He thinks all we need to get out of Paris is a pass from the French military governor. He believes he can get that. Once in Brittany we'll take an old smugglers' route where they don't expect anybody to have a passport."

"What about England?"

"They've become used to all kinds of refugees since Dunkirk. They may check up on us, but if we have nothing to hide, we'll be all right."

"Is Patrick coming?"

"He can't. He's in charge of his office here."

"Where is he now?"

"He went out to meet Dr. Bertrand. A *petit bleu* came from the doctor this morning."

Celia handed Sergei one of the little notes on thin, blue paper that circulated through pneumatic tubes in Paris almost as fast as telegrams.

Dr. Bertrand had scribbled his note by hand, in English.

Dear Mr. McNeill,
   It's imperative I talk to you, but not on the telephone for obvious reasons. I know one place where we can meet without being interrupted or observed. You probably know it, that little café chantant called the Lapin Agile at 21 Rue des Saules. That's in the Eighteenth Arrondissement, near Saint Vincent's cemetery. It will be closed, of course, but I have a key. If I do not hear from you by noon, I shall expect you there at two.

   Yours,
   L. Bertrand.

"I wonder what Bertrand wants?"

Celia waited until Sergei had finished his coffee and then said quietly, "They're here."

"Nazis?"

"Yes. One passed through the Place at dawn on a motorcycle."

"You must get out of this mess as soon as you can."

"So must you."

He was sitting on one of those low window sills that make confortable window seats in old houses with thick walls. He turned his head to look out the window as he answered: "Let's not talk about that now."

"Why not?"

When he didn't answer, she crossed the room and sat beside him.

"Sergei, I'm not going to ask questions, but I know you are in some sort of danger here. If Patrick and Jules find a way to get to England, you must come with me. It's your only hope."

"Is it?"

"That's obvious now. Promise me you will."

She put her hands on his shoulders and brought her face close to his. "Please."

His lips touched hers lightly. Then he was overcome and his arms went around her. His mouth pressed down on hers so hard she could feel the bone beneath the lips. For a moment they clung together with the passion that comes only in moments of despair. Then he gathered her in his arms and carried her into the room where he had been sleeping. They lay on the bed together and time stopped.

When, at last, they drew apart, his hand, still trembling, stroked her hair gently.

She whispered. "Will you promise now?"

140

"I can't promise anything. You'll just have to trust me."

"Sergei, you know I trust you more than anyone else in the world."

He looked down at her without speaking. His eyes wandered across her face as if he were memorizing every feature. He spoke in a low voice.

"Celia . . ."

"Yes?"

"Don't trust me too much."

Patrick loved the Paris street scene too much to use the métro as long as there were buses above ground, but today was different. Today he didn't want to see what was going on in the streets, so he took the métro.

There were only a few people on his train, though ordinarily this would have been the height of the rush hour. They all looked as if they had withdrawn into that invisible, mental life that is our sure refuge from the harsh inequity of the physical world. He didn't like to disturb any of them by asking what station would take him nearest the Rue des Saules. He studied a métro map and chose Lamarck Caulaincourt.

When he came out of the métro he found that the morning had turned into a very Parisian day, low gray clouds and pale, diffuse light which made the Rue des Saules look like a street in a Utrillo landscape of Montmartre. He had been here before, but always after dark and always in a taxi. Now that he saw the place by daylight he could believe the people who had told him it was near the only vineyard left within the city limits.

For this was a village street, and Number 21 was a cottage built in the days when Montmartre was a village on the outskirts of Paris, long before the artists and

141

tourists, bars and brothels took over. There was one modern touch. The small windows were sealed by black-out curtains. They now served to keep people from looking in by day as well as to keep light from leaking out by night.

Patrick tapped on the door. It opened a cautious inch or so and then swung open. Dr. Bertrand beckoned him inside. The moment Patrick crossed the threshold, Bertrand closed and locked the door.

The interior was pure François Villon. A cluster of candle flames thinned the darkness and painted great, black shadows on the dingy walls. Under a low ceiling, the small room was crammed with long, rough trestle tables and narrow benches. At night the benches would be packed with people drinking fine champagne cognac, breathing a pea soup of cigarette smoke and listening to bawdy songs in French that were wittier than most bawdy songs.

They were usually sung by a woman, sometimes by a man, but always in recondite Parisian slang that was impenetrable to most foreign tourists and all French provincials. The others watched the faces of the Parisians and laughed dutifully whenever they laughed.

Something about the place had made it an institution for years, but what was it? The medieval thieves'-kitchen décor? The disarming simplicity of the entertainment? Or the trick it had of making the innocent feel sophisticated?

"I borrowed a key from one of the singers," said Bertrand. "I couldn't think of any other place where you and I could talk so privately as a night club in the daytime. Do sit down. Would you like a drink?"

"No, thanks, it's a little early for me."

"For me, too."

They sat facing each other at the table where the candles burned. Their eyes met above the flames. For the first time Patrick saw Bertrand's face in light coming up from below. This emphasized every sag and crease. He looked much older than he had seemed at their last meeting.

"Couldn't you have come to my office?" said Patrick.

"I want to stay on the outskirts of the city today," said Bertrand. "An occupied city is full of spies and informers. I want the Germans to think of me as neutral and passive. President Roosevelt has made it fairly clear that America has no great sympathy with the Nazis, so I would rather not be seen publicly with an American today. That way I may be of some use later to the anti-Nazi underground that is sure to develop, especially if Pétain takes over."

"Will he?"

"They say it's almost a certainty. . . . I suppose you know why I want to talk to you?"

"I'm afraid I don't."

"Jules!" The name burst from Bertrand's lips explosively. "I haven't seen him since last night. Have you any news of him at all? He has never done a thing like this before."

"I'm afraid it's all my fault," said Patrick. "I kept Jules up most of the night. He only left me early this morning. He said he was going to find a car that I could hire. Of course I assumed he would report to you first."

"Then you expect to hear from him some time today?"

"And I'll tell him to call you as soon as I do."

"But you have no idea where he is now?"

Patrick shook his head.

"I told you about the murder of Aristides Kyros," went on Bertrand. "But I don't believe I did tell you about a theory the Dieppe police have. They think Kyros was killed by another man of mine, Henri Duvernois. He disappeared the night Kyros was killed. There is no other evidence against Henri, but that coincidence is enough to make the police suspect him. That's one reason I'm so worried. Is it possible that Henri is in Paris now and that he has killed Jules?"

"You can write Henri off as the murderer of Jules," said Patrick. "Henri is in Paris, but he himself was killed last night. Jules was with me when Henri was shot."

Bertrand was speechless.

"I'm sorry," said Patrick. "I should have broken this to you more gradually. I wanted to relieve your mind about Jules, and I just didn't think about the shock Henri's death would be to you."

Bertrand shook his head like a boxer in the ring who receives a hard blow, but still manages to keep on his feet.

"Who killed Henri?"

"No one knows yet."

"How do you know Henri was shot?"

"I was there."

Patrick told him the story of last night's events leaving out his own theories about the causes of those events. He muted Celia's experience as much as possible. He had seen before how the nastiness of some crimes, especially kidnapping, seems to rub off on the victim.

Bertrand was visibly shaken. "I can hardly believe all this, and yet . . . do you know I never did like Henri? All the time he was with me I had an odd feeling he was too good to be true, but I stifled that feeling because he was so efficient. . . . I've changed my mind. I'm going to have a fine now. How about you?"

"Just a thimbleful."

Bertrand took one of the candles to light his way to a cupboard Patrick had not noticed before in the darkness. He brought a bottle and two small glasses back to the table.

"Is there no electric light at all?" asked Patrick.

"I don't know. I really haven't bothered to explore. I like candlelight. I think it's one reason people come here."

He held up his little glass and turned it around to show golden highlights in the dark brandy.

"You wouldn't get quite that effect with electric light." Then his mind went back to Jules. "You haven't reassured me. Now that I know Henri was killed last night I can't help wondering if the same thing has happened to Jules this morning."

"I doubt that," said Patrick. "I was impressed with Jules' ability to take care of himself last night."

"That's why I employ him. He was once with French military intelligence."

"So he told me."

"A psychiatrist with a practice like mine needs a man like Jules."

"You have violent patients?"

"No, I was thinking of my patients in government or business who have access to all sorts of political and financial secrets. There is always a danger of my files being stolen because of this. There's a more remote possibility that I might be abducted and questioned rather rudely about some of the things patients have told me in the course of analysis. I feel happier when Jules is with me. When did you last see him?"

"He left me about nine this morning," answered Patrick. "It's only a little after two now. We can't think of him as missing yet."

145

"Now that Henri himself has been killed it's hard to believe that he is the one who killed Kyros," said Bertrand. "I think it more likely that Kyros and Henri were both killed by someone else."

"But who? You're not thinking of those two thugs, Gogo and Pépé, are you?"

"No, they were in jail when Kyros was killed."

"Then you think it's some total outsider?"

"I think it more likely to be someone who was at the villa at the time. I see only one possibility."

"Who?"

"Radetzkoy."

Patrick could only hope that he did not show his surprise. This was a game that must be played with a poker face.

"Did he have the opportunity?"

"Oh, yes. Didn't I tell you there was a period at the villa that evening when all my guests were separated from one another? Suppose Radetzkoy had a rifle hidden in his car. Then all he had to do was to step outside the house and walk a few hundred feet down the driveway. There's a knoll there. From it he could see over the trees to the hollow in the road below where Kyros was looking for his ring. With a rifle he wouldn't have to get close to Kyros. In that very modern, sound-proofed villa the shot would not be heard."

"And you think Radetzkoy then walked down to the hollow and drove Kyros' car back to the villa? Why?"

"If Kyros' car had been missing from the driveway in front of the house, someone might have noticed and started making inquiries about Kyros before Radetzkoy left, but as long as Kyros' car stood there everyone would assume he was somewhere in the neighborhood."

146

"Do you think Radetzkoy is capable of such cold-blooded calculation?"

"A man capable of premeditated murder has to be cold-blooded."

"It doesn't have to be Radetzkoy," said Patrick. "Anyone of your guests could have done it."

"But Radetzkoy was the only really unstable character," retorted Bertrand. "Oh, I know Ambrosine de Varengeville is a little flighty, but I think she stays within the law."

"I wouldn't bet on it."

Bertrand ignored this. "I see Radetzkoy as a subtle and clever cardsharp, and we mustn't forget that cheating at cards is a crime in many countries. Like fortune-telling, it's getting money under false pretenses. The cardsharp gets money out of you by pretending he's playing an honest game when he isn't. The fortune-teller gets money out of you by pretending that he can predict your future when he can't, because the future does not exist. So both are petty criminals."

Patrick could feel his attention sharpening. Was it sheer coincidence that Bertrand was speaking of cards and cheating, fortune-telling and Sergei, all at the same time? Or could he possibly have heard rumors that there was a plan to infiltrate the little group of soothsayers around Hitler? And that Sergei and his curious skill at cards were part of that plan?

"Petty crime often leads to grosser crime, even murder." Bertrand was saying. "It's the first breaking of the tabu against all crime that counts, not the magnitude of the crime itself. If a tabu against murder or adultery is broken just once, it can never become part of your moral equipment again."

147

"Why not?"

"Because tabu is magical thinking, and there can be no exceptions in magical thinking as there are in rational thinking. As long as a tabu is working, you believe that the consequences of breaking it are unspeakable, unthinkable, unimaginable. That's why it works. Primitive people believe that if you commit incest, the crops will fail and volcanos will erupt, but once they commit incest and the crops don't fail and volcanos don't erupt, the tabu ceases to have any effect on them at all."

Patrick rose.

"I suggest you give Jules another twenty-four hours before you call the police. If I see him, I'll tell him to call you at once, but I must get back to Celia now."

"She's still here?" Bertrand was amazed. "I thought, of course, she'd be in England by this time."

"There are certain arrangements we have to make before she can go."

"You've left it too late. She'll never get out now."

"Why not?"

"The state of the roads for one thing. Have you any idea what they're like? I've talked on the telephone to friends who went to Bordeaux with the government. They say it's beyond belief. A mob of civilian refugees and retreating soldiers mixed up with Spanish and Polish workers released by the Ministry of Munitions, all trying to get away from the Germans. Every now and then you see a big car with whitewalled tires cutting its way through the mob. That's the diplomatic corps on its way to Bordeaux. Worst of all is the shortage of petrol, or gas as you would say. I'm told the country is down to a few hundred litres. There may not be any on sale tomorrow."

This alarmed Patrick more than anything else Bertrand had said.

"Then the sooner I get back to Celia the better."

Bertrand lighted his way to the door.

"Adieu, mon ami." Bertrand held out his hand. "I hope we shall meet in happier days."

Patrick turned away, but he could see out of the corner of his eye that Bertrand had not yet closed the door.

Now why is he watching me walk away, down this little Street of the Willow Trees? I wonder how much he really knows about Sergei and how much he suspects? After all, he is a psychiatrist. He must have read a little about ESP. And he talked about magic. He must have heard about the magi around Hitler.

Was he trying to tell me something by innuendo? Or was there something in his mind he didn't want to tell me, and part of it leaked out inadvertently in his talk?

Patrick thought about this all the way to the Lamarck Caulaincourt station without arriving at any satisfactory answers.

There was still no crowd on the métro, but the stale air and incessant noise made him feel a little sickish as he always did on any underground railway in any city.

When he got off he walked up the Boulevard Raspail to the Rue de Fleurus and took a shortcut home through the Luxembourg Gardens.

So far he had seen only a few other pedestrians on the streets. Once inside the iron railings of the gardens there were none.

No lovers wandering down sidepaths. No old men dozing on benches. No small boys sailing toy ships on the round pond that was really octagonal. No small girls asking mothers or nurses questions about the stone images of the queens of France. Only the mist moved,

149

drifting on sluggish air currents among the trees, across the face of the Italianate palace.

Suddenly he felt sadness as he realized that he might be leaving Paris soon. It was unlikely that his New York law firm would want to keep its Paris office open now.

He passed the statue of Mary, Queen of Scots, and remembered the last words she was supposed to have uttered as she boarded her ship for Scotland: *Adieu, charmant pays de France.* . . . Could she have borne that moment if she had been able to foresee the years in prison and the axe at the end?

He had reached the allée that leads to the Rue Soufflot. That long vista was empty, too.

So this is what it would feel like to be the last man on earth. No footfalls but his own. No other human figures but the stony queens of yesteryear. . . .

He paused to light a cigarette.

It was then, when he stopped walking himself, that he first heard footsteps behind him, quick, almost running.

He turned around. He could see nothing there but the mist.

A voice came out of that nothing.

"Monsieur . . . Monsieur McNeill . . ."

Now he could see a tall, young figure, a shadow among shadows in that half-light, but it was not a shadow. It was real.

He looked at it with sheer disbelief. He felt as if all his anxieties had suddenly been made flesh. Were all the things that he had told himself could never happen going to happen now?

For the young man running towards him out of the mist was wearing the long gray greatcoat of a captain in the German army.

16
Luxembourg Gardens

When Patrick saw that he had only one man to deal with he waited quietly. Hardly more than a shadow at first, the young man gained dimension and volume as he drew nearer. He came to a halt about twelve feet away, and it was then that Patrick recognized him.

"Monsieur Konrad? Didn't I meet you at the Hôtel de Varengeville?"

"Konrad von Hohenems." He sketched a salute. "Do not be alarmed." He was speaking in careful, accurate French, but there was still something un-French about it. "I may be in more trouble than you if I am found speaking to you here and now."

And that could be a trick to get me to speak to him, thought Patrick.

Aloud, he said, "Why do you wish to speak to me at all?"

For a moment Konrad was surprised. Then he understood. "It's the uniform, I suppose."

"Naturally. Yesterday you were a civilian and I thought

you were a refugee Austrian or Pole. Now I find you are apparently an officer with the German Army of Occupation, presumably a Nazi. Didn't you expect me to be a little surprised?"

"I am not a Nazi." Konrad looked towards the nearest bench. "If we could sit down? For a moment?"

"Only for a moment. I'm in a hurry, but I'd like to hear you explain this, if you can."

They found a bench under the blank gaze of Catherine de Medici idealized in stone, not the old witch woman Clouet had painted from life.

"It's quite simple," said Konrad. "I am a reservist in the German army. I've been with our Paris embassy in the code department, but now I've been called up. Where I shall be tomorrow I don't know."

Where they were sitting they could see the concrete rim of the round pond and trees beyond. Everything else was lost in mist. Nothing here seemed real. This was limbo, a no-man's-land outside time.

Patrick resisted this fantasy and spoke in his most practical voice. "Do the Varengevilles know you are a Nazi?"

"But I told you I am not a Nazi."

"You are serving in a Nazi army."

"Am I? Or am I betraying a Nazi army?"

"What on earth do you mean?"

"Have you ever heard of the Kreisau Circle of Helmuth von Moltke? Or the White Rose Society among students in Munich?"

"No. Are you telling me that there is an active, anti-Nazi movement in Germany?"

"No, not a movement yet. Just tiny splinter groups underground."

"Working within the system, I suppose? So you can have it both ways? Safe enough during the war and then,

152

if Germany loses, you come out clean and pure, anti-Nazi all the time?"

"You are unfair. We are less than ten percent of the population. Once in power Hitler got over ninety percent of the vote in two plebiscites. What can such a small group as ours do openly? Suppose your country turned into a dictatorship supported by the majority and you didn't like it? What would you do?"

Patrick had never asked himself that question. Thinking about it silenced him for a moment.

Konrad went on: "Please understand we do not see ourselves as traitors to Germany. We see the Nazis as traitors to Germany and to humanity as well. Somehow Hitler must be stopped before he invades Russia."

"You think he will?"

"Of course. The pact with Stalin was strategically necessary but politically disastrous, because it destroyed his stance as a crusader against communism. He must retrieve that stance, and there's only one way he can do it: war with Russia. If this happens, millions of people will die on both sides, both soldiers and civilians. The final consequences are beyond our imagining now. It must be stopped and there's only one way to do it."

"How?"

"Can't you guess?"

The mist was precipitating. In the sudden silence Patrick could hear the slow, steady drip.

"Do you honestly believe the death of one man can change the course of history?"

"In this case, yes. Hitler is a sorcerer who has cast a spell over the German people, but we all know that, when the sorcerer dies, the spell collapses. Have you ever heard him speak?"

Patrick shook his head.

"He is like a burning glass that focuses the diffuse rays of the sun until they set fire to paper," said Konrad. "He focuses the collective unconscious of the Germans to set the whole world on fire. Break the glass and the fire will diffuse itself again as warmth and light. Kill him and his cult will die as an animal dies when you cut off its head. Sometimes I almost think he himself wants to be killed. Doesn't the sacred king die to purify his people in prehistoric cults?"

Patrick had no answer for such bizarre suggestions. It was a relief to him to turn back to the practical. "How did you know that I was going to be in the gardens now? I didn't know it myself a little while ago."

"Madame de Varengeville told me where you lived. I've been following you ever since you left the Place du Panthéon. This was the first chance you gave me to speak to you privately."

"Why are you telling me all these things? I can do nothing to help you."

"It was our friend Ambrosine who suggested that I might approach you."

"She would."

"I beg your pardon?"

"Nothing. Go on."

"There is one obvious difficulty about the project: getting through the guards that surround Hitler at all times wherever he goes. As you probably know there has been one assassination attempt already that failed. This time we have a new plan for penetrating his defenses. You may be able to help us with the plan."

"I can't think of any way I could."

"Not you yourself, but you have a friend who could if he would, Sergei Radetzkoy."

"What on earth are you getting at?"

154

"Only one sort of man from outside Hitler's own circle has any chance of getting close to him today, men like Hanussen, the astrologer, who cast his horoscope."

"I don't know any astrologers."

"Ambrosine suspects that one friend of yours, Radetzkoy, has a gift of precognition and uses it basely to win money at cards. Is that true?"

"I know nothing about it."

"We would pay well."

"No one would do it for money. What you need is a fanatic or an idealist."

"Would there be any hope in appealing to idealism in a man like Radetskoy?"

"I don't know."

"Such a man would have unique opportunities, possibly during seances in a darkened room."

"The problem would be getting out afterward," said Patrick. "What you really need is a man who does not care whether he gets out or not. I . . . but I just can't believe this."

"What can't you believe?"

"That I am sitting here on a bench in a public garden talking calmly about killing a man."

"You are not used to war."

"Not yet. I suppose the idea of killing is something we will all learn to live with before this is over."

"Will you take a message from me to Radetzkoy?"

Patrick was silent.

"You are hesitating? Perhaps I can help you to make up your mind. I have heard from a reliable source that Hitler's magi have already heard about Radetzkoy. They are going to approach him. They will make it rather difficult for him to refuse."

Patrick spoke sharply. "Have you and Madame de Va-

155

rengeville given no thought at all to the possibility that Radetzkoy is exactly what he seems, a clever card-player?"

"You mean a cheat?"

"He may be using a mathematical system," Patrick replied. "Or he may be cheating quite brazenly with marked cards and sleight of hand. Either way he couldn't risk doing what you suggest. There is no undetectable system. Any cardsharp or conjuror can detect manipulation of the cards. Even mathematical systems can be detected by mathematical analysis of play. Radetzkoy would be caught before he could carry out his mission, and he would be hanged. You know they have their own ways of making people talk. He'd tell them everything before he died."

"Have you given no thought at all to the possibility that Radetzkoy might be a true clairvoyant?" answered Konrad. "Ambrosine thinks so. She didn't at first, but now she says there is no other explanation. No trickery, no mathematical system could do the things he does."

"Nonsense!"

Patrick spoke briskly and firmly, but Konrad merely smiled.

"What would you do if you found yourself endowed with such an uncomfortable gift through no wish of your own?"

"You like asking people to imagine the unimaginable, don't you? First you ask me to imagine I'm living under a dictator. Now you're asking me to imagine I'm a clair-voyant. I'm afraid my rather limited imagination is un-equal to either job."

Konrad had taken a visiting card out of his pocket. He was writing a Paris telephone number on it. "Please tell Radetzkoy what I have told you and give him this. Tell him I can be reached at that number for the next three days, but not after that. Time is getting short. Will you?"

"I won't promise."

"At least give him the card and the message."

Patrick put the card in his pocket.

"What first turned you against Hitler?"

"Everything. I wish I could say it was all a matter of principle, but, of course, I can't. Whoever acts from principle alone? My wife is Jewish."

"Do you suppose he has any idea what anti-Semitism has cost him?" asked Patrick.

"Probably not, but I have. For one thing it may cost him the most important move on the chessboard in his game with England."

"And that is?"

"Gibraltar. Franco's mother is Jewish."

Konrad rose. "Please think over what I've said."

He saluted and walked back into the mist.

Instantly the whole thing felt like a daydream until Patrick put his hand in his pocket and felt the card still there.

Halfway up the Rue Soufflot, he knew he couldn't do anything, however slight, to push Sergei in the direction of taking such a suicidal risk. For, if he did, he would never be sure of his own motive. He did not relish the thought of playing King David to Sergei's Uriah the Hittite.

As he came to the Place du Panthéon, he took the card out of his pocket, tore it into tiny shreds, and dropped them in the gutter.

He would still have to warn Sergei that he might be approached by a messenger from Germany.

17
Les Thermes

When the sun was low in the west and there was still no sign of either Jules or Patrick, Celia became uneasy.

"I can understand why Patrick is late," she said to Sergei. "Dr. Bertrand likes to hear himself talk, but I'm worried about Jules. What can have happened?"

"Perhaps he ran into someone who likes to talk, too." said Sergei.

When the bell rang at last, they both hurried into the hall and Sergei opened the door.

Celia, looking over his shoulder, saw Jules and another man half-hidden behind him.

"Patrick, you're late and—"

Her voice died. The second man was Clovis.

"Patrick's late?" said Jules sharply. "Then you'll have to leave without saying good-bye to him. Everything's arranged. You're leaving in an hour, thanks largely to Monsieur de Varengeville."

Clovis smiled. "The pleasure is entirely mine and Ambrosine's."

"I found all the cars I could possibly want," said Jules. "But gas was another matter. I was getting desperate when I had an inspiration. Why not ask Monsieur le Marquis where to go for black-market gas?"

"When he was planning a criminal enterprise, he naturally turned to me," said Clovis. "But I told him he could forget the black market. For the last few days I've been hoarding enough petrol in my big car to get to Brittany at a moment's notice."

"You're going to England, too?" asked Sergei.

"Tomorrow General de Gaulle will be on his way to England. I am joining him there."

"By boat?"

"By plane."

"I thought only military aircraft could cross the Channel now."

"These things can always be arranged," said Clovis. "We keep a small plane at a private airfield in Brittany on some property that belongs to my wife's family. We've got permission from the British to land, possibly because we're bringing with us a chemist who has some heavy water with him."

"What is heavy water?" asked Celia.

"Something to do with a new weapon," said Clovis. "You may be hearing about it before the war is over."

Jules looked at Clovis quizzically. "May I remind Monsieur le Marquis with all due respect that we are not supposed to talk about that?"

"Oh, aren't we?" said Clovis. "I suppose you're right. I just can't get used to secrecy among friends."

Jules turned to Celia and Sergei. "You're in luck. No false names, no forged passports, no disguises. None of those things that are so effective on the stage and so often lead to arrest in real life. Ever since Dunkirk, Eng-

159

land has been hospitable to refugees, but, of course, you'll have to establish identity once you get there."

"These may help." Clovis took some papers out of his pocket. "They're passes made out in your names by the French military governor of Paris, General Dentz. They should get you through any French lines. German lines may be another matter. That's why we must hurry."

"We are going to owe everything to you," said Celia.

"Everything is a big word, mademoiselle."

"But not inappropriate this time, monsieur. If you had any idea what we went through on the road from Dieppe, you'd understand how we feel now."

"You're sure there's room for us in the plane?" asked Sergei.

"It holds five comfortably."

"And the pilot?"

"Ambrosine is the pilot. She's had a license for years and the plane is hers. I assure you she's more than competent."

If Ambrosine's behavior in the air was anything like her behavior on earth, it would certainly be something more than competent. Celia had to remind herself rather sternly that the thing to fear in a plane or a car is not nerve itself but the failure of nerve.

"One more thing," said Jules. "When shall we come to the Hôtel de Varengeville?"

"Why come so far?" said Clovis. "If you can be at the corner of Saint Germain and Saint Michel in exactly an hour from now, we can pick you up there. That's only a few steps for you, and it will hardly take us out of our way."

"We'll be ten minutes early," said Jules. "To make sure you don't have to wait for us."

160

"Our car is easy to recognize, a black Renault, not in its first youth, but well kept." Clovis turned to Celia. "It may be cold, especially in the plane. Do you have a warm coat?"

She shook her head. "We lost all our luggage on the road from Dieppe."

"You should have something warmer and less conspicuous," said Clovis. "White shows up at night. Jules, you'll have to come back with me now and see what madame my wife can find to lend mademoiselle."

"I'll only be a few minutes," said Jules as they went out.

"I wish we could go with them," said Celia. "I'm beginning to feel like a prisoner here."

"It's because we have no passports or *cartes d'identité,*" explained Sergei. "If we were stopped and questioned by a French or German patrol it might make all kinds of difficulties and it would certainly delay us."

"So we're under a sort of house arrest?"

"Only until tonight. That's not long to wait."

"Are we waiting for it? Or is it waiting for us?"

"It?"

"The future." Celia looked towards the windows where the light was beginning to fade. "If only we could know now what is going to happen to us tonight. It seems as if we ought to know when it's so close, just an hour or so. Have you any hunches?"

"Not at the moment."

"You were right about Jules just now. You said he might run into someone, and he returns with Clovis. Was that a guess or a hunch?"

"Call it intuition. That's a useful umbrella word."

"Have you always had intuitions like that?"

161

"More or less, especially when I was a child. You know that game children play, guessing which closed fist holds a pebble or a coin?"

"I remember playing it. You put your hands behind your back with the pebble in one. Then you bring your closed fists forward. The other child has to guess which hand is holding the pebble. As soon as he guesses right, it's his turn to hide the pebble."

"I became unpopular for a while," said Sergei. "Because I always guessed which hand the pebble was in. Then, when it was my turn to hide the pebble, I always seemed to know which of my hands the other child would choose.

"Adults never accept what they cannot understand, but children do because there are so many things they cannot understand. My unpopularity didn't last long. In the end the other children just stopped playing that game with me. They didn't accuse me of cheating. They didn't hold anything against me. They just forgot all about it."

"How did you do it?"

"I didn't do anything. It was just something that happened."

"How did it feel to you when it was happening?"

"You know how it feels when you suddenly forget a word, usually the name of a person or a place? You know the word is there, somewhere in your mind, but you can't retrieve it. It's beyond the rim of conscious memory. If you try to reach it consciously, it eludes you as if another part of your self was opposing its will to the self you know. Sometimes you can almost feel it slipping out of your mental grasp as if someone or something had jerked it away from you.

"There's only one way you can recover a word you

can't remember. Forget it. Let go. Think about something else. Then, like a child playing hide and seek when others stop looking for him, the word pops up in your mind saying, 'Here I am! I fooled you. I've been here all the time.' "

"So you do believe you can remember some things before they happen?"

"Some things, sometimes. It has little practical use because you cannot control it consciously. You never know when it's going to work. And you don't tell anybody, if you can help it. Who wants to be a freak?"

Celia frowned when she heard Patrick's key in the lock. There were so many things she wanted to ask Sergei, but with Patrick here, Sergei wouldn't talk.

Patrick came in slowly,

"Where's Jules?"

"He'll be back at any moment," answered Celia. "He's gone to get a warm coat for me. Oh, Patrick, it's all settled. We'll be off your hands in a few minutes."

Patrick listened stolidly as she told him the plan.

"I'm going to miss you, but it's best for you this way. Just now I met a young German in the Luxembourg Gardens, a friend of the Varengevilles, and—"

"They have German friends? Now?"

"Don't be childish, Celia. Individual friendships don't die overnight when war is declared. They've known this young man for years. He gave me a message for you, Sergei. Have you heard about the little group among Hitler's intimate personal advisers sometimes called the magi?"

"I've heard of them."

"It seems they have heard of you. They may approach you, and if they do—"

The doorbell rang.

163

"That will be Jules." Sergei looked as if he welcomed the interruption.

The coat Jules had brought was of the finest quality, like all Ambrosine's possessions. Black cashmere, soft as butter, with a hood attached which Celia could pull over her pale, conspicuous hair.

"Jules, you should telephone Dr. Bertrand," said Patrick. "He says he hasn't heard from you since last night."

"Then it won't hurt him to wait a little longer." Jules glanced at his watch. "We must leave at once or we'll be late."

It was that hour of dusk that turns into instant night the moment street lamps are lighted. Now, with lamps blacked out, the twilight lasted longer.

The city lay hushed under a darkening sky. It was like the last moments of stillness just before a hurricane.

They walked quickly down the Rue Saint Jacques. At the corner of Saint Michel and Saint Germain they stood with their backs to the iron fence that runs along the eastern side of Saint Michel, trying to make themselves as inconspicuous as possible.

Jules glanced at his watch. "They're five minutes late." He looked down the empty vista of Saint Germain. "They can't say they were caught in a traffic jam this time."

Had something gone wrong at the last moment? No one said it out loud, but everyone was thinking it. Celia wondered how much anxiety people could bear without collapsing? Had anyone ever measured that?

"Here they are." Patrick whispered as if the empty street were full of people who might overhear him. He took her hand and kissed it. "I'll see you in London or New York one of these days."

The car was just as Clovis had described it, an old,

164

well-kept Renault, the highly polished black still preferred to all other colors by those who remembered carriages.

There was another car some distance behind. When the Renault slowed to make the turn from Saint Germain into Saint Michel, the other car speeded up.

Ambrosine was at the wheel of the Renault with Clovis beside her and a pile of furs between them topped with a jewel case. She was driving slowly now, her eyes searching for them.

Jules waved to her and she brought the car to a stop at the curb. At that moment there was a squeal of tires as the car behind her was wrenched around the corner at high speed, careening into the middle of the road and accelerating as if it were about to pass.

Only it didn't pass. It veered and crashed into the Renault with a shriek of ruptured metal and a stunning shock as the two cars ground to a halt locked together.

"Lucien always was a clumsy driver," said Ambrosine.

Patrick snatched open the door of the Renault.

"Anyone hurt?"

Before there was an answer, Jules cried: "Run!"

Ambrosine was out of the car in a flash, abandoning furs and jewels. She took Clovis by the hand and pulled him out of the car.

Jules called to her: "This way."

He ran down a little side street and turned a corner, the others following. He turned another corner and there they all had to stop for a moment because Clovis was panting and stumbling.

Celia had no idea where she was now. There was just light enough for her to see that she was standing next to a high, iron fence. She could hear the sound of running feet coming nearer every moment.

165

Ambrosine turned to Jules. "What do we do now?"

Jules looked at two women, an old man, and a young man limping because of a wounded knee. Was he thinking that only he and Patrick had any real chance of getting out of this? And only if they made a dash for it alone?

If such a thought crossed his mind for a moment he gave no outward sign of it.

He looked across the street at a row of houses with every window dark, every door shut.

He looked behind at the iron fence rising several feet above his head.

His eyes came back to Ambrosine.

"Climb," he said brutally.

She looked at the high fence with horror.

"What about my husband?"

"We'll help him. You first, madame. Step on my back."

He bent forward, bracing his hands on his knees. Another woman might have hesitated or even argued, but not Ambrosine. She placed one hand on his shoulder, another hand on the railing, and stepped up as buoyantly as if she had one foot in the stirrup of a favorite horse. She clasped two spikes at the top of the fence with both hands, hoisted herself up and over and dropped lightly down on the other side, all in a few seconds and without making a sound.

After that performance Celia was on her mettle. It was harder for a man as old as Clovis. Even with the help of the three younger men, he managed to twist his ankle when he landed. He insisted that it was nothing at all, that he didn't feel the slightest pain, but he was limping now.

"Lean on my arm," whispered Ambrosine.

Celia had no idea where she was now. She dared not

166

ask even in a whisper, for survival might depend on stillness.

The place seemed to be some sort of garden, but clouds running before the wind kept visibility shifting between starlight and shadow, so it was hard to be sure what you were seeing or not seeing.

She was aware of grass under her feet and then a pavement. She knew there were trees because leaves whispered to one another whenever the breeze sighed.

Now and then the flickering light gave her a glimpse of sculpture, a weathered face, a distant smile, the motionless folds of a long garment carved in stone. They looked medieval.

Jules led the way into a place where two walls formed a right angle filled with deep shadow. There were bushes in front tall enough to screen them from casual glances. The wall at their backs gave Celia an illusion of security until she remembered that the phrase "their backs were to the wall" applied only to desperate situations.

She forced herself to breathe deeply, believing it would relieve her tension, and it did. She was just beginning to luxuriate in that sense of relief when a great light shattered the darkness, a dazzling searchlight that blinded eyes so long adjusted to the dark.

A voice spoke in French. "Stand where you are. Keep still."

Now Celia could see the faces of the others on either side of her and the tiny leaves and twigs in the bushes just in front of her, but when she looked beyond the bushes she could see nothing at first but the light itself.

It took a few seconds longer before she became aware of the two men beyond the light.

One was young, awkward and innocent, perhaps a peasant boy, for he was obviously uneasy in these sur-

167

roundings. His hand was not quite steady on the submachine gun he was holding. Was this his first experience
of that personal contact with an enemy which is so different psychologically from impersonal shelling or bombing?

There was no doubt about his allegiance. He wore the
gray uniform and the swastika armband, the first Celia
had ever seen.

The other man was a civilian, tall and robust. His overcoat fitted him like a glove. His face was too close to the
glaring light for her to see it clearly, but his posture and
manner radiated an easy authority.

"If you're sensible, you won't be harmed." He was
speaking English now. "By this time I think you all know
or guess why I'm here. I want Radetzkoy."

It was only when she heard the voice that Celia recognized Dr. Bertrand.

"The rest of you have nothing to fear," he was saying.
"Not even my friend, Jules, who, I now suspect, has
never left the Deuxième Bureau."

"Just as you have never left your own intelligence service," said Jules.

For the first time Bertrand was at a loss.

"You knew?"

"Why do you think I was assigned to watch you,
camouflaged as your chauffeur? After your first year or
so in Paris, we spotted you for what you were going to
be: a long-term, resident enemy agent. You were recognized by someone who had seen you when you were a
Nazi agent in Spain in the thirties."

"How?"

"At first we were lucky. Some of your distinguished
patients had the nerve to tell us that you were using the
personal secrets you dug out of them as a psychiatrist to

blackmail them into telling you military secrets.

"The rest was easy. I soon realized that Pépé and Gogo must have been in your employ from the beginning. That ambush of Radetzkoy and mademoiselle on the road to the villa and your rescue of them had to be a little comedy you had planned with Pépé and Gogo in order to win Radetzkoy's confidence, but you took in all of us for a while, even me. Of course you had to keep me in the dark or I would never have been able to act my own part in the comedy so convincingly.

"Afterward I suppose you helped Pépé and Gogo to escape from jail in Normandy. I can't see them doing that without help from outside, and you needed Pépé to kill Henri for you."

For the first time Bertrand was rattled. "You can't have recognized Pépé on the stair in the dark."

"But I did. Two clues. That Marseilles voice that makes two syllables of one, mer-de instead of merde, and that sweet, ambergris smell of his Egyptian cigarettes.

"Of course I asked myself then what possible connection Pépé could have with Henri? You were the obvious answer. You were the only link I knew between Pépé and Henri.

"After that I had no trouble reconstructing the rest of it. You wanted Radetzkoy. He had disappeared on his way to Paris. So had Henri. Were they together? Had Radetzkoy's money tempted Henri, who had already stolen a car from you?

"You knew the address of Henri's aunt. You sent Pépé to find out if Radetzkoy and Henri were there, with instructions to get rid of Henri and rescue Radetzkoy.

"Pépé got rid of Henri, but lost his head and bolted to save his own skin when he heard Patrick McNeill and me coming up the stair. Pépé couldn't risk being found by witnesses with the body of a man he had just shot, and he hadn't the nerve to shoot again without your orders and promises of protection."

"We are wasting time," said Bertrand. "Are you prepared to surrender Radetzkoy to me now? I think you know that he has a peculiar gift which I had a chance to observe at the Casino in Trouville and later at my own villa. I have orders to send him to Germany at once. I can assure you he will be treated with every care and consideration there."

"Is that why you shot him in the knee?"

"That was just bad luck. I didn't mean to shoot him, but I had to intimidate him with a few random shots to keep him away from Kyros' body. If he had got involved in a murder investigation he might have been detained in Dieppe for weeks or months and my orders were to get him to Germany as soon as possible."

"But you admit it was you who shot Kyros?"

"Why not? I had to get rid of him. Like Henri he was getting in my way. Obviously the British had sent Kyros over here to keep me from sending Radetzkoy to Germany where his gift of precognition might give us a strategic advantage." Bertrand peered into the shadows until he saw Sergei. "Are you ready now, Monsieur Radetzkoy?"

Sergei took a step forward into the light. "I'm quite ready."

"No." Celia ran to him. "You're not going with Bertrand. That's insane. The man is a murderer and a spy. You can't trust him and he won't trust you. This is suicide."

He took her hands in his and spoke in a hushed voice just above a whisper.

170

"Don't you understand that I have pledged myself to go if I have the chance?"

She answered in the same half-whisper.

"But that was before Bertrand had any reason to suspect your good faith. Now if you can't produce the kind of information they want, they'll think it's willful, and what will they do to you then?"

When he didn't answer, she went on: "You were never coming to England with me, were you?"

"No."

"Do you remember what you said? 'I'll get us both to England in a few days.'. . . Was that a trick to make me go where you thought I would be safe? Didn't you know by that time that I didn't want to go anywhere in the world without you?"

"Dearest Celia, I warned you once not to trust me too much."

In the last few moments, Jules had been inching forward almost imperceptibly. Now Bertrand noticed him.

"Stay where you are, Jules. My young friend here has an itchy finger on a trigger."

Whether the boy with the submachine gun understood the words or not, he understood the tone of voice. He raised his gun a little higher and gripped it more firmly, glancing from right to left.

As the boy looked towards Sergei, Jules slid his revolver out of his pocket. He knew he would have only one surprise shot, so he aimed at the light.

With a crash of breaking glass, they were plunged into darkness again. Eyes that had been adjusted to the glare of the searchlight were sightless for a few moments.

"To the fence!" cried Jules.

It might have worked if the clouds had not parted at

171

that moment. The crystal starlight did not bring definition or perspective, but it diluted the dark so you could see movement.

Bertrand swore at the boy in German. "For God's sake, fire!"

The boy stammered. "B-but . . ."

"Stop all of them except the Russian. We want him alive."

Jules took careful aim and fired at the boy's right hand.

"My hand!" he cried out in German, but he did not drop the gun as Jules expected. He clenched it more tightly and squeezed off a burst of machine gun fire involuntarily without aiming at all.

The quiet of the night was ripped apart by high-pitched stuttering. Bullets ricocheted from the old, stone walls of the garden. One hit Bertrand in the breast. Another hit Sergei in the throat.

The boy who had fired was as dazed as if he had been shot himself. Jules had no trouble taking the gun away from him.

He had more trouble making Celia understand that Sergei was dead. She was on her knees, holding Sergei in her arms, staring at the crumbling old walls as if something about them frightened her.

"Jules, what is this place?"

"Les Thermes? Traditionally the baths of the Emperor Julian. Probably a Roman frigidarium built in the reign of Caracalla."

"Would you call it a Roman ruin?"

"What else could you call it?"

L'Envoi

PARIS

1978

The Smoking Mirror

After the war, Celia passed through Paris on her way to other places twice, but she had no occasion to linger there until 1978. She wrote to the Sûreté, for news of Jules Yersin and received no answer. She then tried the Préfecture, the Ministry of War, and the Ministry of Foreign Affairs. All three assured her that their wartime records contained no mention of a Jules Yersin.

At this point she went as near to the top as she could, the American ambassador. He consulted a friend on the French General Staff, and at last a reply came through.

There was no such person as "Jules Yersin." That was a nom de guerre of Colonel André Flavigny, formerly of Military Intelligence and active with the Resistance during the German occupation. He was now a member of the Chamber of Deputies, living at an address on the Île Saint Louis.

Celia wrote him a short note and received a telephone call inviting her to dinner the next evening. If agreeable he would call for her at six o'clock.

On the telephone his voice had sounded exactly as it had thirty-eight years ago, but, when he arrived, changes were apparent. His hair was entirely gray now and would soon be white. Time had cut weary lines in his face and given his eyes an expression somewhere between cynicism and good-humored resignation.

Yet he was still slight and alert with a lively sense of comedy, and his welcome was so warm that during the first few moments she had to fight the tears that come so much more easily to the old than to the young.

So she was Madame Patrick McNeill now? And there were two children and a grandchild? Good. And that dear Patrick? Ah, Jules was indeed sorry to hear that he was dead.

She still thought of him as Jules. If there was a personality that went with the André Flavigny name, it was not a personality she knew.

He had a little, open car outside, just right for a June evening in Paris. He drove her towards the Bois. The streets were familiar and unfamiliar. The old buildings had kept their shape, but some of them had been sandblasted to preserve their fabric. Perversely, she missed the lovely chiaroscuro of accumulated grime.

In her day, there had been so few privately owned cars in Paris that there was always a place to park. Now, in districts like Montparnasse, cars were so thick on the ground that they were parked on sidewalks in long rows.

They came upon Armenonville suddenly around a corner. It stood under a violet sky in a pastoral setting where the last thing you expected to see was a fashionable restaurant. It was sited so artfully that at' this twilight hour it seemed to float in the mist of greenery around it, like a villa in an impressionist painting.

There were tall windows of shining glass and soft

lights widely spaced. Beyond the glass was slow movement, one man waiting on one table of early diners with the unhurried formality of a minuet. Through an open window drifted an echo of nostalgic music. It was as near Cinderella's dream of fairyland as one is likely to come on earth.

Not until they reached coffee and cognac was the old familiarity reestablished between them.

During dinner Jules had given her little tidbits of news. He had seen to it that Sergei's body was decently buried in a churchyard near Paris. Bertrand had been wounded, but not killed. According to Vichy courts, there was not enough evidence to prove charges of murder and espionage against him, so he had been imprisoned on various lesser charges in France during the war, and he was now said to be still alive in Germany.

Ambrosine de Varengeville lived in Brittany, a very old woman, paralyzed by arthritis. Her nephew had married a Californian, and the present Marquise de Varengeville was another kettle of fish altogether.

Clovis? He had been killed in a London air raid.

"Anything else you want to know?"

"Lots of things. Why didn't Patrick recognize the scent of Egyptian tobacco as you did when Pépé passed you both on the stair? That always bothered him."

"The censor in the human mind does not always let a smell reach consciousness. Not because the human sense of smell is atrophying, as some people used to think, but simply because we don't like to admit we're that animal. Patrick felt something familiar in the air, or so he said at the time. He just couldn't identify it consciously."

"Did it never occur to Bertrand that Sergei might be a British agent using his reputation as a clairvoyant to penetrate the Nazi organization?"

177

"Of course it did, but Bertrand believed in Sergei's clairvoyance and thought it could be conscripted. You have to remember the Nazis were adept in the art of coercion. Bertrand relied on that."

"What was Kyros really? Sergei's protector and line of communication with England?"

"Why do you think he talked as if he were hostile to Sergei when you first met him at the pension?"

"To hide the fact that he was Sergei's ally?"

"Of course. There was a lot of playacting in this affair. Why do you think a police officer as high ranking as Inspector Grosjean was on the pier in Dieppe when you came off the boat? He had been told to waylay a White Russian with a Nansen passport who would claim that the passport had been stolen. He was to make the Russian conspicuous by questioning him suspiciously and putting him under town arrest. This was to make the German agents who watched the pier during the phoney war believe that the French had suspected Sergei of Nazi sympathies. Such a belief made it much more likely that Bertrand, one of the chief Nazi agents in France, would feel free to approach Sergei with a proposition once he had observed Sergei's precognition in action at the casino in Trouville."

"Is that the real reason Sergei wanted to go to Trouville that night?"

"Probably. He had been told in England that Bertrand went to that casino almost every evening and that it would be a good place to make the contact."

"Sergei said once he learned a great deal from that first meeting with Bertrand. What do you suppose he learned?"

"That Bertrand suspected him of using ESP when he played cards. What else would explain a psychiatrist's sudden, intense interest in the uncanny skill of a card player? And then Sergei himself had to complicate everything by falling in love with you."

"Did he?"

"You know he did." Jules paused and stared at Celia. "You're looking at me now as if there were some question I haven't answered. What is it?"

"Der rauchende Spiegel," she said. "The smoking mirror. What does that mean?"

Jules took a twist of tissue paper out of his pocket and unfolded it on the tablecloth.

Lying among the folds was a ring she had seen before, a gold-rimmed cartouche containing an intaglio carved in desert-colored agate. There was a tiny, human profile with a prominent nose and a head crowned with . . . what? Plumes or flowers?

"How did you get that?"

"It was among Bertrand's things when he was arrested."

"How did he get it from Kyros?"

"Did Bertrand shake hands with Kyros when Kyros turned up at the villa?"

"Yes. How did you know?"

"That would make it easy. Any pickpocket will tell you that, if your ring is loose, it can be slipped off the finger gently during a handshake, so you won't notice the loss until you look down at your hands, especially when you have a lot of other things on your mind, as Kyros did."

"But why did Bertrand want the ring?"

"He didn't want anyone else to get hold of it after Kyros was killed. Bertrand was a member of a group who used these rings as recognition signals. Because of this, Kyros had hoped the ring would recommend him to Bertrand. Unfortunately it had just the opposite effect because Bertrand already suspected Kyros of being an enemy agent.

"These rings had far more political significance than the silver death's-head rings worn by S.S. officers. Anyone wearing one of these rings was likely to gain instant admission to the occult group closest to Hitler himself. Other groups of initiates called themselves the Luminous Lodge or the Thule Group or the Black Order, but this most secret group of all called itself the Smoking Mirror."

"Why?"

"Can't you guess?" Jules touched the profile engraved on the stone with one finger. "This little fellow, the god Tezcatlipoca, was called the Smoking Mirror, because he could foretell the future and bestow that gift on others.

"It is believed by some that his worshipers consulted a magic mirror when they wanted to see the future. Not a glass mirror. One of polished metal. When an ordinary man looked into that shining mirror, he saw the present, but when a seer looked into that same mirror, it became clouded with smoke to his eyes—smoke that churned and fumed like the mist in the crystal ball of our own soothsayers. It was then he saw the future."

"So the Smoking Mirror is the clouded crystal? And the smoke is the kind where an adept can see the shadows of coming events, ghosts of the future, memories of things that have not yet happened?"

Jules nodded.

"You don't believe that, do you?"

"I don't know." Jules shrugged. "Sergei had something. What it was, we'll never know, but he did have something. Perhaps the future is as real as the past. Perhaps we could all see it, if we really wanted to."

"Why don't we want to?"

180

"Our Freudian friends say we have amnesia for unpleasant memories, and what could be more unpleasant than a memory of one's own future?"

"Because it would destroy free will?"

"Because it would destroy hope, and we can't live without that."